HEART'S KEEPER

DARK WORLD MATES

OLIVIA RILEY

CHAPTER ONE

Tryth

The sky lit red as the sun peeked over the horizon. A dull orange like the waking eye of a titan against the foreground of a dark landscape beyond. Far off, sharp rocks and wild, twisting trees with fiery red and yellow leaves and purple vines scattered for miles in every corner. Closer, down below, were the outer domes and buildings of the inner haven. There was a breeze, warm, not yet terribly hot, but Lana knew as the sun rose the temperature would spike, and the wind would eventually sting her skin.

She had gotten used to the heat over the years, but having been away for so long on their last mission, she had a feeling it would be uncomfortable at least for a few days. Just like the first time she had come to Tryth.

At least this time she was more prepared. No more sulking in the dryrooms where it stayed fairly cool, next to the food storage and water banks. Though she might end up there for an hour or two by midday just for a break.

But it wasn't so bad just yet. With the sun barely up and the nice breeze, she could stand to sit on the terrace just a little longer. Xini had left out the tea set for her when Lana had first come up, just like the many times before as had become routine over the years. Despite being gone for nearly a year and a half, Xini hadn't forgotten, and Lana had been extremely grateful to find her favorite spiced tea brewing on the groundmat, ready to be savored. It was a nice familiarity that Lana needed.

She and Xerus had only returned a night ago, so exhausted both physically and mentally from the mission that they had barely said a word to their housekin, those who kept their home safe and clean when they were gone and served them when they stayed. They had gone straight to their room and slept the night and most of the day away, only getting up once to eat and going right back to bed after, with Xerus curled up against her back as always, nestled firmly in their den with no light to wake them and little sound to stir them from sleep save for the low hum of the air vents.

Lana wished it had been a peaceful sleep, but endless dreams had made that impossible. Only Xerus' hand caressing her arm and his voice, turned soft in her ear, gave her comfort and allowed her to fall back into a calm sleep. She must have been talking again or maybe kicking as sometimes happened, but Xerus never seemed to mind. Especially when she started sleep-talking in the vrisha tongue instead of her native one. It seemed to amuse him, listening to the things she said.

Lana closed her eyes and smiled at the thought, but the smile didn't last when she remembered waking up to find him gone. Xini had said he'd been away for some time, out hunting in the far territories of their home. It wasn't unusual per se. He'd gone hunting many times before, even sometimes taking her with him, though she was never good at it.

But this time made her feel...wary. He didn't usually leave her in the mornings, but that shouldn't bother her and, mostly, it didn't. What did bother her was the tension she'd noticed in him ever since they had left Jara—the planet they had been sent to for their mission; the place they had been for so many months. She wondered if it had put a toll on him. It had certainly left a mark on her.

But even as they ventured close to home, he had seemed off, and still she worried. She had wanted to talk to him when they woke, and that was when she had found herself alone. It was no matter. She could wait until he returned.

Lana took a sip of her tea and watched the shadows play over the valley as the sky brightened from a deep red to a peach color. Her hand shook slightly, but she thought little of it as she set her cup down carefully. Her eyes drew down to her naked legs, and she stared at the tanned skin marred now by a few scars. She had many all over now, made from living in a harsh environment and having a sharp-skinned mate. There were no fresh ones currently, and she should be thankful for it, but sadly, it reminded her of how long she had been away and how few private moments she and Xerus had gotten toward the end of their mission. It was hard to be intimate when one was so focused on saving a whole race from being lost.

Not extinct. Lost. Lana learned after Jara that there was indeed a difference. But perhaps the Jaras didn't see themselves as lost. Rania, their queen, said it was for the best, but after so many years of being accustomed to other cultures and learning to take a step back from her own opinions and accept the difference in others' lives, this had been the first time Lana couldn't do it. She still felt like she had failed them, though according to the Jaras—and to Xerus—she had not.

Lana found herself staring out at nothing, deep in thought, when she heard the soft shifting of feet drawing close.

"Forgive my intruding," said a vrisha voice in a gentle hiss behind her. Lana turned and saw it was Xini. She bowed her head, the light of the sun shining off her sleek black horns. "Would you have me bring you some food, *Risa?*" she said. Lana tried not to flinch at the title. She'd told Xini many times to call her by her name but *Risa*, meaning "my queen," slipped out every so often.

"Maybe in a bit," Lana responded half-heartedly back in vrishan. Xini watched her for a moment before approaching closer.

"Something troubles you," the vrisha said matter-of-factly. Lana smiled, albeit a bit sadly. She had never quite figured it out, but the vrisha she'd become close to had grown very good at guessing her emotions. She theorized it was in the sound of her voice.

"I'm just still trying to recover from the mission," Lana said.

"It was difficult."

Lana's throat tightened. "Yes."

"I will call for your predomis."

"No, it's fine. Let him hunt."

Xini's tail swished back and forth, meaning she was thinking about what to do. After a moment, she decided to sit beside her. "Will you tell me?" she said after a pause.

Lana looked at her, knowing she probably looked more concerned than she wanted to. It wasn't like she couldn't tell Xini. Missions were not at all confidential. The vrisha worked as a pack, as a community, to try and deal with all manner of issues. If Xini didn't find out from her, she would know of it from council meetings. Lana just wasn't sure she wanted to concern her or others with her wellbeing. A vrisha queen needed to be of sound mind, and if she was "ill" in any way, it affected the whole haven. But talking it out might do her good, though she wished it was with Xerus instead.

"When we first heard about what was happening on Jara," Lana said, "I was so afraid that it was the parasite again. That Spectre had somehow come back. Or that we had somehow missed it there. Though the council claims the planet had been deemed safe from harm back when vrisha were first fighting the parasite off. Reports from vrisha who'd come from there said the Jaras were acting strange, and fights were breaking out. Soon the fights turned to battles and there was the start of a war. When we got there, we soon learned it wasn't the parasite." Lana looked off in the distance, watching the leaves flicker and glow like flames in the light.

"What was it?" Xini asked.

Lana looked back at her. "They were changing."

Xini tilted her head. "How so?"

"They were beginning to hear each other's thoughts, know each other's emotions." Lana shifted where she sat and frowned. "Like one singular mind."

Xini rubbed at one of her horns in thought. "A hivemind. I have heard of races being one from the start but never of one turning into it. How very interesting."

"Interesting." Lana laughed. "No. Disturbing." An itch grew on the inside of her wrist underneath her scaled cuff, and she scratched at it without thought. "We tried to help them stop the fights. To try and find a way to bring them back but..." Lana jerked her head one way in a sort of vrisha headshake. "Even after we helped stifle some of the fights, the queen said it was time they embraced the inevitable. I tried to reason with her, but they'd made up their minds, and me and Xerus just watched them slowly fade away, losing their own individuality. I could never imagine such a thing happening, it was just so..."

They sat in silence for a moment before Xini said, "You do not like their decision and so it still bothers you."

"Yes," Lana spoke softly. "That and..." She looked across to the jungle, past the buildings of their haven.

"And?"

"I think it might have affected Xerus too somehow," Lana said honestly.

"How so?"

Lana wasn't sure exactly how to respond. She thought it over, then said, "He seemed distant after...like he was distracted by something. Our whole trip home, I could tell something was off. He was so quiet. And when I tried to speak to him, it's like he didn't hear me. I would have said something sooner, but I was also still reeling from the whole thing." Lana sighed, then drank down the rest of her tea and set the cup aside. "This was not how I was hoping to come home."

"But at least you are home," Xini stated. "And now you can take time for yourselves. Talk to him. Tell each other of your concerns and fears. You do not have to take another mission for some time if you do not wish to."

Lana smiled at her. "You're right. And I do plan to talk to him when we can find a moment together."

Xini gave her a quick bow, then took the tea set as another house-kin, Syris, entered the terrace.

"*Risa*, your predomis has returned," he said, flicking his tail.

Lana and Xini locked eyes. Xini nodded her head and showed the tips of her fangs in a vrisha smile before turning away. "Thank you, Syris," Lana said as she rose from the groundmat. The wind picked up, catching in the tight braids of hair which fell down Lana's back and through the strips of kelva, a strong, leather-like hide, around her thighs. The heat and rock-dust pricked her skin and stung her eyes. Time she went inside.

Syris bowed his head and stepped away as Lana entered through the open door into darkness and the somewhat cooler interior of their home. She moved carefully down a flight of stairs till she reached the central chamber, a circular space with a domed ceiling. A map of Tryth's solar system displayed from above, and the walls showed stone etchings of wildlife and landscapes. The floor, made from dark bronze and stone, had several vrisha designs and pictures like hieroglyphs which could be translated if one understood. Lana knew them all now by heart. The lights—deep red and orange cracks of stone the vrisha called stonelights— glowed dimly around the dome's outer circle. At the center of the room was a low-lit flame in a large bowl with seats surrounding it. It was where housekin gathered to talk. A place of unity for the vrisha of the house where one needed to speak and be heard; the heart of their home. A home that sat above the haven as its own center.

No one sat there now, and Lana passed by the fire to walk down a hall opposite. There were few doors in the haven or within their home, but staircases and short bends or screens kept things private and hidden. She went down one lone staircase until she came to the bottom of her and Xerus' private den. As she walked around a thick screen, the glow of the stonelights above brightened as she passed.

The den was empty. Lana stopped near the middle to look across at her and Xerus' bed—an oval-shaped pit cut into the floor with a mat and pillows scattered within. The fabrics were soft but incredibly durable as a vrisha's spikes couldn't cut easily into them. Everything was smooth yet hard. Even the walls and floor were made of a soft but tough rock that the vrisha created from the flow of lava rock. It reminded her of the stones found on a beach, made smooth from years of sand and water.

Her eyes slid across the room and studied the subtle etchings along the walls then moved over to a globe map to one side that showed the vast area which the vrisha had explored. On another side were a few plants Lana had been caring for and collecting data on before her mission, tended now by housekin. There was a table next to the plants filled with Xerus' gadgets and tools and a cabinet housing the few pieces of clothing she wore along with her one set of vrisha armor they called *grivhide*. It was what she wore at her queening ceremony and to council meetings. The armor, made from those vrisha who had fallen, hung to one side along with a crown of horns Xerus had made especially for her. She thought fondly about that now. He had given the crown to her at their coupling ceremony. A smile played on her lips when she recalled it being the only thing she adorned when they lay together in their bed after. It made her think of the dreams she had before she'd come to Tryth. How wild and alive she felt with him.

From a doorway to one side, Lana heard the light trickling and splashing of water. Along the top of the passageway was the flickering of light from the water's reflection. Quietly, she stepped over to the door. The scent of coffee hit her, and she closed her eyes, smiling. Stepping through into the passage, she slipped down a short set of steps before entering the bath chamber.

Within a long, rectangular bath, Xerus stood, his back to the door. Wafts of steam floated just above the surface of the dark water, breaking against his body. He hadn't noticed her yet, and Lana took that moment to watch him carefully as he glided around the pool. His tail weaved lazily behind him, creating small ripples through the water. Even now, Lana could only stand in silent awe of him. Of his dangerous beauty. Pale orange light lit the room like the light of dawn, and in it, Lana could make out the brilliant deep red of Xerus' scales as they shined. There was the hint of dark purple stripes along his side from the scars he had acquired some years ago. His horns, though twisted and angled slightly differently than the others', were full and thick and sharp as ever. The spikes along his back were a bit jagged if one looked hard enough, but it was of little issue. His lithe body was a sight to behold, even after all the years, still powerful and feral as he moved gracefully along the bath. What fear it had pulled from her long ago was no longer of any concern. Still, her heart raced all the same; for the love of him that she believed could never be broken.

Eventually, he turned and saw her watching him. He grew still as they locked eyes, and Lana became so lost in the heat of his red and black gaze for a short moment that she couldn't speak. Xerus' expression, though stunned to see her there at first, quickly calmed, and the glint of eagerness showed in his eyes as he gave her his sly smile.

"I wondered where you had slipped off to when I returned to find our bed empty, kissala," he said in a low voice.

"I thought the same thing when I woke up to find you missing, my domis," Lana said, returning his smile.

Xerus' smile fell slightly as he stopped in the middle of the bath. "Forgive me. I was restless."

"The hunt helped?"

Xerus bowed his head. "In a way..."

Lana looked down at the water and approached the edge of the pool. "May I join you?"

Xerus huffed, his tail curving along the water. "Would I ever tell you no?"

Lana shrugged then began to unclasp her Kelva garments from

her thighs and shoulders. "I would hope not, but then if you ever needed to be alone..."

"I would never deny your presence."

"Even after having to endure it for so long?"

Xerus hissed a laugh. "I never tire of it if that is what you mean." He reached out an arm to her, and, as Lana stood naked at the edge of the bath, she slowly dropped into the water and moved across to be beside him. As if done unconsciously, Xerus's tail curled across her back, pulling her closer to him. Lana let out a slow breath and closed her eyes as she felt his rough scales brush along her skin. She placed her hands along the underside of his ribs and pressed against him, letting her forehead rest against his chest.

"I missed this," she said softly. "With how little time we had together on Jara..."

Xerus' face came down and brushed against the side of her head. His hands rose and gripped her shoulders gently. "I understand entirely. It was difficult, with everything that happened."

Lana kept still for a long moment, then rose her head to look up at him with concern. "I wanted to talk to you about that." Her hands slipped to his back, rubbing gently. "You seemed distant when we left."

Xerus tilted his head as he eyed her. "Did I?"

Lana nodded. "Did it bother you?"

"Did what?"

"You know...what we witnessed...with the Jaras."

Xerus' eyes flickered over her. He lifted his hand to brush a knuckle across her jaw. "No, kissala, it did not. It was what they wished. We did what we could for them, and I am content to know our mission was completed to the best of our ability. Even if it was not how we would have imagined it to end." His hand rested between her neck and shoulder, and he caught her eyes once more. "Now, I am only content to be home with you, Risa."

Lana gave him a small smile though she was still uncertain. "I am happy to know it." Her smile dropped. "But you would tell me if something was bothering you."

"Of course."

"And there's nothing?"

Xerus seemed to think it over, then said, "I admit I have had...moments of restlessness. But I cannot place their motive or reasoning. There are thoughts that wander; urges for something I can't grasp. But it is hard to say what they are or why. I feel a pull, a need for something I cannot see. It is confusing." He tilted his head in a shrug. "It is likely due to being away for so long. Perhaps I yearned for home more than I thought." His eyes brightened as his hand slipped under her chin, forcing her head up. "Craved to be here with you and not having that moment has made me...tense."

Lana studied his expression and knew he was being honest. Still, she worried, but she let the uneasiness go and slipped her arms around his waist to press her hips against him, feeling his wonderful heat.

A low rumble settled in his chest.

"And what of you?" he said. "Tell me, my queen, what troubles you?"

Lana let out another slow breath. "I ...I guess I'm just upset about the Jaras. I didn't want to witness them losing themselves like that. It felt like...giving up."

Xerus grunted. "Or letting go and accepting the inevitable."

"There must have been another way. Something we could have done."

Xerus shook his head. "I don't think so. Not anything we could have found in time. But eventually, they will learn to cope. Learn to survive."

"I would never want to go through that," Lana said honestly. "I would rather die than go through that."

"You will never have to worry about such a thing."

"You're right. Perhaps in a few thousand years when humans evolve into some other form, then we will have to worry. Unless..."

Lana shivered, as memories suddenly flooded her mind. "Unless something like Spectre came back..."

Xerus' expression went dark. "Even if something did, I would never allow it to take you from me. You would never be lost to me like that. Not ever." He nearly hissed. The parasite was always a delicate subject for him, and Lana tried to be careful when bringing it back up. Right now, she wasn't doing the best job, but her worries made it difficult not to talk about it.

"What about you?" Lana said. "You don't think there is anything that could ever control you or the others?"

Xerus' hand fell to rest against her throat, and his mouth twitched in that amusing sort of way. "No. We are not so easily controlled, as you well know."

Lana's eyes fell from his. "But there is always the possibility of something...something we didn't see or never even imagined."

Xerus' hand slipped around the back of her neck, rubbing gently. "What is it you fear?"

Everything, Lana thought. *Anything that would take you from me.* She didn't voice her thoughts, but they spoke in her mind with alarming clarity, making her stomach twist. Why, after everything, did she feel so wary? They had many other missions before but this one left her realizing just how easy everything could change.

Lana glanced up at him and smiled. "I'm not afraid. If I'm with you, I have no reason to be."

Xerus nodded in agreement.

"I'm just overthinking," Lana continued. "But we can put the mission past us now. What's done is done."

"What's done is done," Xerus repeated. His hand fell to rest now on her waist. He gripped her and brought his face down to settle along the curve of her neck. He nipped her playfully, then nuzzled, his rough mouth grazing her soft skin. "And we are here now. Be with me here," he whispered in her ear.

Lana closed her eyes, her arms folding around him as she pressed her body fully to his. His rough scales grazed against her, and the heat of him enveloped her fully in his embrace. His hands moved from her waist to her back, his clawed fingers trailing down her spine, making her shiver. She let out a shudder of breath and forced her mind to focus on him and nothing else, on them together in this moment, letting the past slide away and the future be shrouded from sight. They were home, and as Xini had said, they could stay for however long they liked. No more missions for a long time.

The thought of this calmed her somewhat. She relaxed into him, kissing his shoulder and chest, tasting the droplets of water mixed with the tang of his skin. A low growl like a soft purr escaped him and she felt herself being lifted up. As she rose partially from the water, Lana clung to his shoulders and allowed him to move her across the bath in order to set her down against the pool's edge. As he led her down to lay on her back, Lana couldn't help but smile. She tugged him down to her and kissed his mouth, flicking her tongue against him, and, in response, he met her with his own, sliding partially between her teeth before retreating and lifting his head. He moved downward, and Lana felt the heat of his tongue graze against her neck and breasts, then down to her stomach. She tensed as she felt him between her thighs and let out a hiss of breath. Ever since he learned of how sensitive she was in that particular spot (and how it made her react), he favored it, delighting in how her body moved and writhed, loving the taste of her. Lana almost didn't believe him at first, but he convinced her quickly in the beginning when he put great time and care into the act. And it didn't take much to make her body burn.

Lana arched and lifted her head, a loud moan ripping from her throat as his tongue curled and flicked against her in all the right ways. She shuddered as her body throbbed, goosebumps forming along her skin. Xerus lifted his head and moved to settle back on top of her, but before he could do so, Lana sat up and gently pushed him back.

"My turn," she whispered, dipping back into the pool. She led him into a more shallow part of the bath where the water only came to his thighs. She pressed a hand between his legs and felt his cock already freed from his protective inner pocket and hardened, ready for her. She glanced down to see the length of him just above the water, curved and dark. A smirk played on her lips as she lowered herself and heard him hiss with excited pleasure. She remembered her first time going down on him and how he had crumbled after. She certainly felt like a queen then, seeing him in awe of her. Just like the first time, she grabbed the base of him and pressed her lips to his head and slid her mouth around him. Another hiss and low groan escaped him. His hands tangled in her braids, gripping her head, tail swishing behind him in anticipation. She moved on him as she had many times before and, just like those many other times, he went still, trying desperately to keep his release at bay. For all he could endure, this always defeated him.

The telltale growl and shudder of his body told her how close he was. But before he could let himself go, he released her and forced her back. "No, not like this," he said. "Not this time."

Lana looked up at him at first in surprise, then smiled and rose. Without turning away or leaving his gaze, she slowly moved to the stairs of the pool. Xerus watched her like a predator studying its prey, then followed her over, his eyes alight with fire as he met her. Lana sat herself down on the last step where the water only came up an inch, and laid herself out, resting her head on the lip of the bath. Xerus stood above, his eyes drinking her in before he lowered himself on top of her. She could feel the heavy thumping of his heart, his muscles tightening, the smooth scales of his stomach pressing against her, the heat once more consuming her. He gripped her wrists and moved her legs farther apart with his own thighs. Lana lifted her knees and hooked her feet behind him before he pressed against her and slid himself fully and deeply inside. Lana gasped, arching her back and lifting her hips. The feel of him was so familiar now it didn't faze her when he moved quickly and without pause. His hunger for release could be felt with each thrust and, with no barriers between them, Lana let herself be consumed and possessed. He gripped her hard and moved wildly against her, locking her in place though she writhed under him. Noises escaped them that neither tried to stifle. Water splashed around them unnoticed. Lana saw and felt nothing but him, and when her body tightened and shattered once more under him, he soon followed, his heat filling her. He slowed his pace as each breath came out a ragged grunt, his body shaking.

Xerus placed his weight on her just enough not to crush her. He looked down at her, making sure she wasn't hurt or uncomfortable. Besides a few cuts from his scales which she'd barely noticed, she was fine. Lana clung to him for a long moment before turning her head up to look at him.

"God, how I missed this," she said, letting out a shaky laugh. "Promise me we don't have to go away for at least a little while. That we can stay here."

"It will be so," he said in a low voice. He lowered his head, hiding his face above her. Lana lowered her arms to pat the sides of his ribs.

"When we go to the next council meeting, we will give them our report and request a pause on all outer missions," she said, petting his side. "There will be plenty of things to fix here at our own haven anyway. We focus on home now."

Xerus said nothing. Lana felt his breath slow and his heart settle back into its usual pace. He moved, slipping from her and lifting himself up so that he could meet her gaze.

For a mere second, Lana thought she caught a dark shadow in his stare, but it was quickly gone as he blinked with his inner lids and grinned down at her. "A fine plan, my queen."

He sat back beside the edge of the bath and pulled her up to cradle her against him, bringing his knees up, wrapping her in the protective sphere of his body. "We have all the time and nothing to keep us away."

CHAPTER TWO

Though Lana would have gladly spent the rest of the day with Xerus in their room, being home didn't mean their work was over. Now off-mission, their focus lay solely on the running of their home and haven where several thousand vrisha lived. When they were away off-world, such responsibilities went to those stationed below the queen and her predomis—the head housekin. All matters were talked over and dealt with between them in the central chamber of the house. When Lana and Xerus returned and were rested enough, matters of the haven moved back to them. Anything that happened while they were away was reported to them by the housekin.

Lana made her way up to the heart of their home, expecting to meet with Xini and others to go over everything they had missed in the last year and a half. Xerus would meet up with her later to discuss their future plans. His brothers—Tyrus and Rysha—were away on separate missions but had left a message for him. Lana had only met with them a handful of times in all her years on Tryth as their missions always seemed to overlap. The brothers were more welcoming to her than she had first expected though they liked to poke fun every so often for her soft skin and "prey-like appearance," whatever that meant. Xerus said they thought she was cute—which in vrisha terms was not a compliment.

Lana remembered the mixed reactions to her arrival well enough. Some were intrigued, most were shocked, a few weren't so happy. But with Xerus' retelling of their fight from Lazris and the death of Spectre, more grew convinced and accepting, especially as time went on. As Lana learned the culture and learned to respect their ways—to think as they did and understand their world—the better her relationship with those around her became. Being the queen of a haven—a city cut into the dark mountainside along sharp rocks and twisted trees—took more time to accept, but Lana grew more comfortable with the status, especially with Xerus' help. The queen, after all, was not some all-powerful ruler but more of an overseer of the city, protecting its laws and helping to shape it into a better community. Like a mayor of a town. And her haven was not so big, not like some. It was much more manageable, and the people took a liking to her.

Lana took the last steps up to the central chamber, expecting to find a group of housekin waiting for her, but instead, she found Xini alone. When she turned to face Lana, her eyes looked troubled.

"Where are the others?" Lana asked.

"The meeting has been canceled," Xini replied. "There is someone who wishes to speak to you. A scout from a seaside haven. She has been waiting a long time and will wait no further. I tried to tell her you only just returned home and needed time but..."

Lana frowned. "Where is she now?"

"At the shipped. I was coming down to tell you."

"What does she want?"

Xini shook her head. "She did not say but claims it is important. She came here some time ago asking for you, but you were gone on mission, so I turned her away. I could not force her to go this time. She is very insistent."

Lana's brow furrowed, and she slipped past Xini, heading down another passageway toward the shipped. "Let Xerus know to meet me at the dock. I will meet with her."

Xini bowed her head and disappeared down another hall. Lana turned and made her way up to the shipbed located at the highest point of the haven. She climbed till she reached the tunnel entrance and saw the light of the outside at the end. Ahead, with the light of the sun, she could see a lone ship docked at the center. The rest of the shipbed was empty with her and Xerus' main ship already stored in a building across the way along with a few extras of their choosing. The closer she got, the more she could see two other housekin along with Syris talking to a female vrisha Lana didn't recognize. Her skin was a dark purplish-red, and she had a slender build, her black horns shining in the sunlight.

As Lana approached the end of the tunnel, the female saw her and stopped mid-conversation. The others looked around and bowed their heads. They stepped aside so that the lone woman could walk past and connect the distance between them.

"You are one difficult person to get a hold of, Dr. Hart," the female stated.

Lana froze mid-stride.

"You know me?" Her eyes flitted over the vrisha woman with confusion. No, she never met her. Very few knew her full name. Some didn't even know her first name, most calling her Risa.

"I know of you," the woman corrected. She placed a hand to her chest. "My name is Xilya. I was part of the mission to find and help destroy the parasite that took over so many worlds. I was captured by a large multi-planet civilization. I've met humans within their territories. Shall we talk inside?"

Lana blinked at her, trying to process everything she just said. She became very aware of the heat, the sun now at its peak. Sweat was already breaking along her brow and between her breasts as her skin grew hot.

"I—yes, let's go inside." Lana was still in shock at the information the woman had just dumped on her as she turned back for the tunnel. A large, advanced civilization was no longer anything she was surprised by. But humans in another alien's territory? How? and why?"

The woman, Xilya, followed her back down into the home. When they reached the central chamber, Xerus was there talking with another housekin. When they saw Lana enter, the housekin bowed to Xerus and left. Xerus turned and locked eyes with Lana first before glancing behind her to the vrisha female. The pair stood several feet away from one another, and Lana allowed them to size each other up and display their status. A common vrisha greeting between strangers. Xilya kept her head slightly bent, studying Xerus calmly while Xerus kept his head tilted back, his tail swaying indifferently behind him. Their nostrils flared, and their eyes dropped to the ground before Xilya finally hissed and bowed her head.

"Predomis. Risa," Xilya said. "I have been trying to get a hold of you for some time." She made a gesture toward the inner circle of seats and fire pit. "May we sit?"

Lana glanced at Xerus and nodded her head. "Yes, let's."

As they sat, with Xilya taking a seat opposite them, the fire at the center grew larger, and the room's light dimmed. Xerus eyed Xilya across the fire, the woman returning his stare.

"It so happens I just received a message from my brothers about you," Xerus said to Xilya. He tilted his head. "They said you have been trying to contact us for a long time. But you would not say why."

"Yes," Xilya said. "Specifically trying to meet with Dr. Hart."

Xerus was very still as he regarded her, only his tail brushing against Lana's leg in a protective caress. His eyes narrowed on Xilya with suspicion. "It is odd for you to involve my brothers instead of seeking the head council in order to send such a message out."

Xilya's tail twitched behind her. "I did try the council and they refused my request."

Lana's eyes widened. "Refused you? To only send a mere message to us?"

Xilya's gaze turned to her. "They thought it would compromise your mission."

Both Lana and Xerus were taken aback.

Lana recalled what she said to her moments ago outside the shipped. "Because it involves my kind?"

Xerus looked at her in surprise, and Xilya dipped her head. "They thought if you knew of the situation involving your people, you would not be able to focus and ultimately complete your recent mission." She let out an irritated hiss and rubbed at her neck. "If there was ever one time I truly loathed vrisha customs, it has been these last several cycles. A vrisha's mission is always of the utmost importance as you both well know. It cannot go uncompleted. I spent many years away trying to finish mine, thinking I had failed. By Rikasha, we cannot even return if a loved one falls ill, we must continue on. I was fully aware and accepting of this law until very recently. I knew even if I got a message out, you still would not be able to return. But I believed you had the right to know at the very least." Xilya dropped her hand and reclined back. "But the council saw it as a problem best left till you returned. I had no choice but to wait." From a small pocket sewn into the hide of her kelva pants, Xilya revealed a slender oval-shaped device. "Much has happened since you left." She set the oval device above the fire and there it floated until it began to glow as if burning hot. The orange glow took over the room until beads of light appeared around the chamber, like floating bits of embers. An outsider might just think it was a pretty light effect, but Lana knew it now as a map showing a specific part of their universe. One particular set of lights lay in a cluster above them, growing larger.

"For several years, I was imprisoned within a mining planet run and owned by the empire known as Xolis," Xilya said. "There, I became friends with one of the ruling class of this empire who had been exiled. They are known as the nillium."

From there, Xilya told them everything she could about this large, multi-system empire known as Xolis, and the nillium and of the various races that called this empire home. When asked if anyone had ever heard of such a place, Xilya said, "There might be veterans who have heard mention of such a place, but it is otherwise outside our scope of knowledge. I was tasked to find the parasite past the known sphere of where it was found, to make sure it was not lurking in the farther reaches of our map's sight. Xolis was just a little way beyond the farthest any vrisha has gone. I was found by enforcers of Xolis on one of their planets. There were too many for me to fight alone and so with shame I was forced into servitude. But some years spent within the mines lead to the discovery of a ship. From there, I and the nillium Ryziel and a native of the mines called Nar worked to fix the ship." Xilya's gaze fell to Lana. "And a couple of cycles after, we met the pack of humans."

Lana leaned forward, hand sliding to Xerus' thigh. He took her hand, slipping it into his own, rubbing his fingers over her palm. "How did they get there?"

Xilya told them about Grayhart and the group of explorers who'd traveled too far for their own good. About their capture, then being saved and housed in a Xolis facility before being taken to the mining city—Lethe Maws. She told them about the men who died and the women who were stolen away. About the nilliums' desperate attempt to repopulate and how the human women played an important role. Lana sat silently listening, growing cold at the tale Xilya told.

When Xilya finished, Lana cleared her throat and shifted in her seat, glancing at Xerus for a brief second before returning to the vrisha female. "But they did get out, right? All the women?"

"Correct," Xilya replied. "I returned several of them to a lone human base at the edge of their territory where they contacted their organization known as Grayhart. Then returned here to speak with you—only to find you already gone on your mission."

"Several...but not all?"

"Not all." Xilya shook her head. "Two decided to stay with my nillium friend on a planet hidden from Xolis, home to an ancient race. They are safe there despite all that has and is happening now within the empire."

"And what is happening there exactly?" Xerus asked.

Xilya turned her eyes to him. "Based on the information I've been sent by my friends, the nillium rulers have been fighting for power. The first appointed after the prince's death was assassinated, and from there, fights and deaths have been many. But their issues are nothing yet for us to be concerned about. What is concerning are the hunters who've been searching for human women."

Lana sat up straight. "The nillium are still looking for them?"

Xilya tilted her head in a shrug. "More or less. Though recently, their focus has been swayed by the change in power and the struggle to keep the foundations of their empire intact. It is a man named Vesra who has been aggressively sending out hunters in search of your kind in hopes of gaining power and wealth over the nillium. I received a message from my Xolis friends only a little after I arrived back on Tryth that this Vesra had deployed some of his best hunters to go looking for Earth women. There was little I could do at the time save meet with the council and try to persuade them to bring you home. As a mere scout, I did not have the power to leave and set off for human territory myself or bring others to give aid. But as queen, you would have that ability to make such a decision."

"It's been a year and a half since you've returned and heard of this," Lana said. "How do we know these hunters haven't already found other humans?"

"I've been staying in contact with my friends since then," Xilya explained. "Through Xolis networks and spies, they have been keeping a close eye and ear out for any news of the hunters and Vesra. So far, none have yet to return with any humans. We thought perhaps they had given up for the time—that either they had failed to find any or that the unrest in the cities turned their focus away—but a few cycles ago, several new ships were reported being sent out with a small army of Vesra's men. They have been out searching for some time and may be near to Earth's systems as we speak."

A low grumble rose in Xerus' chest. "What do you propose we do?"

"Those women I left on a human base were told to warn others about the hunters," Xilya said. Reaching her hand out, she turned the map over the fire so that the beads of light drew in closer. She pointed to one spot of light within a small cluster. "This planet is where I left them. It was a small military base, they said. From there, they were to talk to the heads of the base after making contact with their leaders from Grayhart. Unfortunately, though I kept a way to contact them, I have not heard anything from the women since I dropped them off. But I am confident that they would have warned the others, giving them time to prepare. Despite that, humans are not well equipped to deal with those from Xolis. The empire's technology far exceeds their own. If they do find them, it could be very bad. I had hoped that when I found you here, I could persuade you both to assemble a few soldiers, and we could stop those from Xolis before they had a chance to get close to any human settlement." Xilya turned the map again, bringing the systems back into view.

Lana rubbed her fingers over her temples, thinking. "Only one problem with that. There are dozens of planets in Earth's systems. The territory spans pretty far, probably even farther since I've been gone. How do we possibly track ships from another civilization and keep them away from planets spread across several solar systems?"

Xilya scratched idly at the side of her jaw. "I worried about that too and thought it over for some time. Eventually, I spoke with those still in Xolis and asked them to send me a blueprint for a tracking device to hone in on a specific energy source. The ships in Xolis are run on a mineral called Ionx. The ship I brought here was one of these and carried some left in its engine bank. For several cycles, I worked on this tracking device so that it could detect Ionx bursts in space which would indicate a driving ship. If we were to gain close proximity to Earth's territories, the tracker would have a wide enough span to detect ships from a certain distance."

Lana's eyes widened. "That's rather impressive," she said honestly. "And would make it a lot easier."

"I have my ways," Xilya said with a proud flick of her tail.

Lana looked to Xerus, who sat quietly in deep thought. If they left, if they gathered a group of soldiers to take with them and try to bring down these hunters from Xolis, by vrisha law, it meant they were taking on another mission. A mission outside their home.

Lana was one breath away from saying "no." But she swallowed the word down hard before it could be free from her lips.

"Allow me and my mate to discuss this privately," Lana said instead. "We would like a night to think over everything."

Xilya watched her with interest for a long second, then quickly reached out and grabbed the floating map. The beads of light went out as she placed the device in her inner pocket. "Of course. You will need time to prepare." Xilya stood. "I will wait for your decision."

Lana rose after her. "You may take a guest room here if you wish. We will call on you in the morning."

Xilya's eyes shifted between her and Xerus before she bowed her head and turned to leave.

When she was gone, Lana looked back over at Xerus, who gazed back at her. She took his hand, and he rose to stand beside her. He searched her eyes for a long moment, and Lana could guess what he was thinking. She didn't want to speak more of it in the central chamber, so instead, she tugged him gently to follow her.

CHAPTER THREE

When they entered the garden, the sky was a pale orange as the sun fell closer to the horizon, and a few wisps of pink clouds covered its yellow light. Steam rose in tendrils along the ground, climbing up walls to disappear. The garden was situated in an eastern courtyard surrounded on one side by walls of dark brown rock from the mountaintop, and the rest closed in by sections of their home, specifically the housekins' quarters and one of the kitchens. Lana had planted many of the flora there herself back when they had only just moved in and were taking time to make the place their own. There were large purple flowers in the shape of starfish and plants with long leaves covered with red spikes. Druumils—large bee-like insects with wide wings like a moth—fluttered about between the flowers and crawled along the body of a well-kept statue of Queen Epris and her predomis, Servus, the haven's first, at the garden's center. Below their feet was a bench, but neither Lana nor Xerus took a seat. Instead, Xerus stood in front of the statue and watched as Lana paced before him.

"This news troubles you," Xerus said after a moment.

"I don't know what to think," Lana replied. "It's all so sudden." She let out a small, frustrated laugh. "I haven't even thought of what might be happening back...back on Earth and its bases. I was so wrapped up in everything here. I never thought...never thought something like this would happen."

"It was only a matter of time," Xerus said, "till the humans started finding other races. There is much in the universe that even vrisha know little about. And we've been traveling much longer."

"Maybe if humankind realized how unprepared they were to go poking their noses far outside their own territories," Lana muttered bitterly, "this wouldn't have happened."

"Perhaps, but it couldn't be helped." Xerus tilted his head, his eyes traveling over the garden and back over to her. "And they've learned a dire lesson. Regardless, they may need our aid."

Lana sighed as she continued to pace. It wasn't fair. They had only just returned home, and who should muck things up but her own kind. It wasn't fair.

But for all their problems, not all of the human race could be to blame. Though she'd been content to not return home ever since Lazris, to let the human race go on without her, she knew there were still innocent lives that could be harmed if she didn't try to help. The vrisha were the most powerful and ferocious fighters she'd ever known. And she had the ability to utilize a small portion of their forces. Could she really say no and turn her own kind away just so she could stay and hide in her home with Xerus and never look back? Could she live with herself if she said no and let innocent people be taken from their own homes?

No. As badly as she wanted to stay here with her mate, her conscience wouldn't allow her to shun all of humankind. She thought of Dahlia and Nicole and those on the base. She and Xerus had saved so many back on Lazris. And saw just as many die. If these hunters found a human settlement, there would be bloodshed; men slaughtered, and women torn from their families. She knew she couldn't ignore the threat any more than she could have ignored their enemies years ago.

Lana stopped pacing and turned to face Xerus. "We have to help. I can't let them just be taken. Not when I have you and other warriors who could stop them."

Xerus' mouth twitched as he moved toward her, connecting the distance between them. He placed a hand on her shoulder, then let it fall along her arm, fingers trailing down her skin, until he had her hand in his, and he set her palm to the center of his chest. "Where you go, I go."

"It will be dangerous. We might face a species we've never met."

Xerus snorted. "I fear no one."

Lana studied his face and pursed her lips. "You're actually excited about this, aren't you?"

He gave her a slow smile. "It has been a long while since I've had a good fight and a good foe. Plus, I miss seeing the terror in their eyes."

Lana gave him an exasperated sort of look. "In your foe's or in a human's?"

Xerus' smile widened. "Both."

Lana rolled her eyes and tugged her hand away, though a smirk peeked from the corner of her mouth. "You're awful. You're not supposed to want to instill fear in every living thing."

"I disagree. I think that's exactly what I was made for."

Lana smiled despite herself. " Well, you failed miserably with me, didn't you?"

Xerus' eyes narrowed, tail swaying. "If I recall, you were quite terrified the first time we met. And for a long while after."

"You took some getting used to, I'll admit," Lana stated, with her head tipped back as she regarded him. "But now you're no more terrifying to me than that sprisal plant behind you. All sharp and spiky on the outside and gooey soft on the inside. I'd cuddle you like one of the mirrul found lounging on the terrace walls and sleep just fine."

Xerus huffed. "A mirrul, really? I don't even have fur."

"No, but you purr like one when I do this." Lana raised her hands and grazed her fingers along Xerus' sides and back, messaging the pressure points between his back muscles and spine. Xerus' pupils widened, and a soft rumble stirred in his chest before he gripped her wrists. His fangs peeked out ever so slightly, and his eyes brightened. Lana let out a small laugh. "See?"

"Careful," Xerus said. "That is a dangerous tactic. It may force me to fight back."

Lana arched her brow. "Oh? And what is it you think you can do?"

As Xerus bent his head, his hand traced down her back, and Lana felt his mouth against her ear. As soon as his tongue flicked against the outer shell of her earlobe, Lana shuddered, goosebumps spreading over her body, heat stirring in her center.

"Not fair," Lana stuttered.

She heard him let out a low hiss as his mouth trailed down to her neck, and he flicked his tongue over the skin before giving her a sharp nip with his teeth. Lana let out a soft groan, then quickly pressed against him, wrapping her arms around his waist.

She groaned again into his chest, this time in irritation, then looked up at him, resting her chin against his scales. "I don't want to go."

Xerus looked down at her and brushed a hand along her head. "I know. And I don't wish to see you unhappy. Let us hope we can scare away these men of Xolis enough that they will never come back. Then we return here."

"One more mission," Lana sighed. "Then you're mine alone. And we aren't leaving again. At least not so soon."

Xerus grinned, showing off his shiny black fangs. "Agreed."

Lana went to pull away, but Xerus held her still. "We should get back and call on the housekin," she said. "We still need to have our meeting."

"They can wait," Xerus replied. He led her to the bench at the statue's feet and sat down, placing her on his lap. Unclasping the ties of her kelva bottoms, he nuzzled her ear and let out a hiss of breath. "Let us enjoy what little time alone now we have."

* * *

After their discussion in the garden, they had their meeting as planned and afterward took dinner together on the terrace. As night came, they slipped back inside their home, Lana still thinking heavily on everything they had talked about and the news they had learned. Only once they were back in their room did she allow herself to wind down and try to clear her mind, putting the thoughts away for the next day.

The den was dark and relatively silent save for a low hum and the soft trickling of the bath in the room beyond. With no windows to see out of, no light or sound from the outside disturbed the chamber. One might feel claustrophobic, but the den was very open and well-ventilated. All was calm as Lana lay quietly, letting the day fall from her mind into nothing. With Xerus beside her, she slowly felt herself beginning to fall into a deep sleep.

Appearing from seemingly nowhere, an odd scent filled the air. Lana's eyes fluttered open as the scent hit her. Brow furrowed, she looked over at Xerus, who lay sleeping peacefully. The odor was subtle but disturbing enough to put her on alert. She sat up and looked around but saw nothing out of the ordinary. She sat for a quiet moment, wondering if it was just a trick of the mind. When the scent didn't disappear, however, Lana rose from the bed and stepped out to stand bare at the center of the room.

Everything was as it had been, but Lana circled the room regardless, searching. She went into the bathroom, and nothing was wrong there either. Yet the odor remained. She started for the stairs, and the scent grew.

The curious scent of tobacco.

There was no tobacco on Tryth. Not like that on Earth. And the smell was distinct. She knew that smell vividly. And the memories it brought.

She climbed the stairs and walked down the short tunnelway. The smell was overpowering now. She froze in the middle of the passage when a sound carried down the way. The voices of several people were talking over a static background. A radio.

There were no radios on Tryth either. Confused and concerned, Lana walked the rest of the way down the passage until she came to its end. But instead of entering the central chamber, she found herself in the middle of her father's living room.

That definitely wasn't right. She looked around and saw his favorite chair by the window and the radio on the table next to it. The faded red rug on the floor was falling apart, threads poking every which way. Outside the window, Lana could see the dock and her father's boat bobbing gently. In a bowl by the chair was a cigarette still burning, a slender trail of smoke coming out one end.

Lana stood there for what felt like hours just looking around the empty room, and in that time, it never occurred to her to think she was dreaming. Eventually, she called out, "Hello?" to anyone who might be near, but her voice came out like an echo drowned out by waves. She thought she heard someone in the kitchen, and she moved toward the door. As she walked inside the kitchen, the room turned back into her and Xerus' den.

Lana watched Xerus sleep, and a soft red light began to envelop the room. When she turned her head in the direction of the bath, she saw instead a large glass screen with several men behind it, staring at her. She recognized every single face, and her heart dropped at the sight of seeing the generals, her old friend Jacob, and Cole Kingsley looking back at her. They watched her. No, studied her. And they smiled.

Cole came up close to the glass and grinned. "He's truly a magnificent specimen, isn't he?"

Blood slipped from his nose, but he didn't so much as wipe it away. Lana shook her head, unable to understand. Blood trickled down the glass screen until it gushed in torrents, blocking the men from sight. Lana felt her heart racing out of control. She went to shout back at them and, as she turned her head, found Xerus crouched behind her. Eyes red like hellfire, bloody teeth bared. Rage and emptiness in his eyes. His tail whipped back, and, with a violent snarling roar, he leaped at her, and Lana screamed.

Gasping for air, Lana woke. Sitting up, she looked down at Xerus, and her heart leaped in her chest. He was still sound asleep.

Trying to calm her breathing, Lana carefully got up, the air hitting the sweat along her back, chilling her, making her shiver. She moved toward the bath and stopped, placing a shaky hand over her eyes.

She'd had dreams about the past before but not something so vivid as the one she just had. Not in a very long time.

It was the stress of going back. Of remembering what had happened, that was all. They rarely talked of Lazris, but with everything that was happening now, it was bringing back unwanted memories.

Lana dropped her hand and looked back over at Xerus once more. She thought again about their trip home after Jara and their conversation in the bath. He'd said he was restless. That he felt urges he couldn't explain. She suddenly wished she had asked him more about it. Though he had put her mind at ease then, she still felt anxious. It wasn't like him to be restless for no reason. She wished she knew what he was thinking.

Lana exhaled slowly and turned back for the bath. It was better to put it out of her head. They had more serious matters to worry about now. Tomorrow they would have to prepare to leave; to prepare themselves for a return to human civilization.

And hope my kind don't try to kill Xerus and imprison me while we try to save them, Lana thought bitterly. She hadn't spoken with a single person since she left. Who knew what kind of trouble she and Xerus were getting into this time?

CHAPTER FOUR

When Lana woke the next morning, she found herself alone once again and Xerus missing from their den. Choosing to believe he had decided to wake early to gain a fresh start on all that needed to be prepared for their journey, she quickly washed and dressed and headed for the central chamber above. When she didn't find him there, she made for the terrace where they sometimes took breakfast. There, Xini had prepared a groundmat with various dishes and spiced tea underneath a small canopy. The sun's light was only just peeking over the horizon, and a few tyili—long-necked birds with horned beaks—sung down in the trees below. When Xerus was nowhere to be seen, Lana asked Xini if she had seen him.

"He went out before the break of light to hunt," she responded.

Lana took a seat down on the groundmat and frowned. "Oh." It was odd that he would go out a second time in a row and not tell her. And to leave the grounds now when they had so much to prepare for was also very strange. She looked up at Xini who quietly went about checking the plants along the terrace wall and shooing away a couple of mirrul that chittered at her before disappearing down to a level below. She seemed quiet and kept her eyes averted which made Lana feel suspicious. "What is it?" Lana asked.

Xini glanced her way, then turned back to another potted plant. "Did you talk to your predomis about his distance?" she asked suddenly.

Lana didn't respond at first. She took a sip of tea and set the cup down before saying, "Yes, we talked. He says he has been restless but doesn't know why. That he's felt a pull to something but can't explain what. He claims it's due to being away for so long, but I'm not sure."

Xini flicked her tail and tilted her head but remained quiet. Lana traced a finger along the rim of her teacup and watched her. She could tell the vrisha female seemed more rigid than usual. "Why do you ask, Xini?"

Xini looked back at her, and her eyes made Lana feel a slight jolt in her stomach.

"I'm sure it is nothing to be concerned about," Xini said. "But he did seem a little off when I saw him go."

"Off how?" Lana asked.

Xini looked around the terrace as if trying to find the right words. "He seemed...distracted by something out in the jungle. He kept very still, watching down below for a long while before he eventually left. I tried to ask him before he passed the house gates if he needed anything from me but when he turned to look at me..."

"Yes?" Lana asked after a long pause.

Xini's eyes fixed with hers. "He looked at me like he didn't recognize me. Then his warning scent filled the air."

Lana's eyes widened. He only ever excreted his pheromones when there was dire danger. But he had never ever used it on a housekin or even those within the haven. Any other time was a sort of heat scent, and it was only ever with her. The scent reminded her of the smell of fresh coffee but with others, it was not so pleasant and drove them to fear.

"Do you think maybe he was dreaming? Perhaps he was sleep-walking?" Lana asked. Though she had never once encountered him or any vrisha sleepwalking and didn't even know if they did such a thing.

Xini shook her head. "No, I don't think so."

"Maybe it was too dark, and he didn't recognize you?"

Even with the look Xini gave her, Lana knew it was a foolish explanation. Vrisha could see very well in the dark.

"I'm sure it was just some sort of misunderstanding," Xini said. "He said nothing to me and headed out to the jungle after."

Lana grew worried. "Maybe we should go looking for him?"

"If that is what you wish, I can gather a team to find him."

Lana thought it over seriously then shook her head. "Let him be for now. If he does not come back by midday, send someone to search. I wouldn't want it to look like I didn't think he could take care of himself out there." Because she didn't want to embarrass him like that. Xerus had always proven himself to be more than capable of holding his own. And the only threat in the jungle was a gris—the squid-like monsters that were equipped with poisonous barbs—but he was very unlikely to encounter one this close to the haven.

"So be it," Xini said. She bowed and moved to let Lana eat alone. She turned her head one last time to regard her. "I wouldn't worry about it too much, Risa."

Lana nodded her head as Xini disappeared back inside, then turned her gaze over to the jungle far below and frowned. She sipped her tea and ate what she could from the meal Xini had placed out (as it was rude to waste) watching the sunrise. When she was ready to head back inside, she had a housekin call on Xilya to meet her once more in the central chamber. Before she rose, she eyed a small cup of *sivas* but knew she wouldn't be able to stomach the drink and so guiltily let it be. Usually, Xerus drank it for her as the first time she tried she was nearly sick but, as he was gone, it would have to be savored later. She placed the bowls in a neat line at the edge of the groundmat and gave her thanks to Veradis and Rikasha with a bow toward the sun, as was custom after the first meal, before leaving the mat and entering the house.

Once inside the central chamber, Lana found Xilya already there waiting for her. When they locked eyes, Xilya bowed her head, and Lana gestured for her to take a seat.

"Your predomis does not join us?" Xilya asked as she sat across from her.

Lana crossed her hands on her lap and tried to keep her expression blank. "He is away at the moment but should be back soon."

Xilya gave her an odd look. And rightly so. It was not normal for a queen to be without her predomis when discussing important matters, especially involving a mission together. But thankfully, she did not press the matter and instead kept silent as the lights dimmed and the fire brightened.

"Xerus and I have talked it over. We will begin assembling a team and a ship to take us to human territory. We will try to stop these hunters from Xolis if we can."

Xilya bent her head as she regarded her. "How soon can you assemble your forces?"

"I will have to let the council know of our decision first. Once I talk with them, I can start gathering a team as soon as tomorrow and be ready to leave within a couple of days."

Xilya scratched at her jaw and nodded, satisfied enough. "Good. The sooner the better."

"Because we have no way of knowing when these men from Xolis will show up, we will probably have to make camp on one of the bases or settle near one in space," Lana explained. "So we will need a lot more supplies. I can gather what we have here and call for more aid from the council if need be."

"That would be wise," Xilya said. "We should bring extra fuel as well. We may have to make several jumps in case my tracker detects them early on and we are forced to make chase. Also, I forgot to mention yesterday that I made a copy of the pulse tracker the hunters use to find and trace humans. It is merely a precaution in case we're too late and they find women and decide to hide on some planet undetected. The women I brought back were generous enough to lend me their DNA signature in order to recreate it. I think it will be of good use if we are to fail. "

"It's good that you've taken great care to plan this out," Lana replied. "I wouldn't worry about failure. I am fully confident Xerus and our soldiers will find them in time."

"Let us hope," Xilya said.

Lana studied her for a long moment, then said, "What brought you to want to help so much with this, just out of curiosity? You could have left the women at the base and never looked back. What made you want to save these humans?"

Xilya reclined in her seat as she stared down at the fire. "As I mentioned yesterday, I met them back on Xolis. One, in particular, I got closer to than the rest. Her name is Aly. When she told me about you and what happened with the parasite, I was highly intrigued. Especially learning you had been made queen." Xilya shrugged and flicked her tail lazily to one side. "I got to know her and became fond of her as a friend. When she was stolen away, I helped to save her and the others from the nillium. They were so very innocent, but they endured." Xilya's eyes narrowed, and her voice turned low. "It angered me to see what the nillium did to them." Her sharp eyes flicked upward to meet hers. "And for no reason except that they could give them children." She hissed and rubbed at her neck as if recalling a memory. "Also I want revenge on those Xolian bastards for entrapping me for so long. They don't get to have these women too. They can go extinct and rot away for all I care."

Lana's heart softened at Xilya's words, and she gave her a small, albeit sad, smile. "Thank you for caring about my kind and helping them."

Xilya dipped her head. "I will feel great pleasure in seeing our warriors rip the hides of these hunters when we find them."

"You are not alone in that," Lana said, thinking of Xerus' comment yesterday in the garden and his excitement for a fight.

"They will feel and know what a vrisha is capable of," Xilya said, swinging her tail around and flaunting the sharp, pointed tip.

Lana could imagine what such a fight with the vrisha would look like well enough. It would likely be a slaughter more than a fight, but Lana felt no mercy for the men who threatened her race. And as vicious as the vrisha were, Lana had grown used to their savagery over the years. She was just thankful they usually used it for the greater good and not to conquer and destroy anything and everything they encountered. Though they weren't completely without their faults (they had a few wars in the past to take control over certain territories, and some had gone rogue, attempting to assassinate their queens), most had a more open mindset than might be expected.

They talked over their plan once more and agreed that their best chance of confronting the Xolis ships was when they were closer to human territory. Better to wait for the hunters to come to them instead of them searching endlessly across a specific portion of space spanning from the Xolis systems to the humans' in hopes of finding them. When they felt they had talked enough about it for the time, Xilya left to prepare and gather the necessary items from her ship, and Lana made her way to a callroom to join a meeting with the council which took place at certain intervals of the day.

The meeting didn't last long, and Lana was able to get their approval for extra supplies. The queens of other havens even offered her extra aid should she need it, and Lana was exceedingly grateful for the gesture, saying she would consider it if need be. By the time she had left the meeting and exited the callroom, it was a little past midday, and Xerus still hadn't shown up.

Anxiety beginning to eat at her, Lana made her way to the front courtyard and was about to call on a few housekin to go in search of him when she spotted Xerus near the gates of their home. Letting out a short sigh of relief, she started toward him, then froze when she really took in the sight of him, and her heart dropped to her stomach.

He was covered nearly head to foot in dirt and blood. And there were gashes on his side and arms; what she could only assume were bite marks. Lana stood there dumbstruck for a few long seconds before slowly closing the distance between them.

She was about to ask what happened but was made silent by the look he gave her, a sort of sneer, and this time, she stopped a few feet away from him.

"Xerus?" she said nervously. She dared not get closer, and Xerus did not move to draw near, his body still as the mountain. "Xerus...are you all right?" she asked, growing more concerned.

He blinked several times at her as if confused. Then, as if nothing were wrong at all, his expression changed.

"Lana." His eyes brightened and his body relaxed. He looked delighted to see her, as if he'd only just run into her after a nice walk.

Lana's brow furrowed as she stepped cautiously to his side, her eyes searching his face. "What happened?" she said, trying to keep the panic out of her voice.

Xerus tilted his head slightly but didn't seem to notice nor feel concerned for the fact that he had blood and mud all over him. His gaze only reached her.

He drew up a hand and brushed his fingers along Lana's cheek. Lana stilled as his hand fell to her throat and rested there a moment before dropping. "I...was restless. Forgive me. Were you waiting long?"

Lana opened her mouth, then closed it, not sure how to respond. "It's no matter," she said finally. "I didn't want to disturb your hunt." She tried not to glance down at his body, but it was too difficult. She'd seen him hunt before, but he was rarely messy about it. Judging by what she saw now, he must have not only killed his prey but torn it apart and—noticing the blood on his mouth—eaten it too.

It wasn't that he didn't take prey to eat. But always, it was skinned and cooked first. And if there was one thing Lana knew well from the beginning, Xerus never cared for raw meat. If he caught something, it had to be cooked. So seeing him now and knowing he'd just gone out and made a meal of something without preparation was a little more than disturbing.

Lana glanced around and noticed a few of the housekin watching curiously nearby. It wasn't like they didn't hunt either (it was a vrisha pastime after all, though many preferred to hunt in couples or in packs), but judging by their confused stares, they too knew something wasn't right.

Lana turned back to Xerus and took his arm, tugging him toward the house. "Let's get you cleaned up."

* * *

She waded in the bath, placing herself at Xerus' back, using a rough washing block to scrape away the grime over his scales. "You really didn't know you'd been gone so long?" she asked as she rubbed his back.

"No. I somehow lost track of time." He turned his head to eye her behind him. "I'd thought I'd only been away for a couple of hours, not half the day. I must have been...a little too focused."

That was an understatement. Lana washed his back without a word. She let him dip under the water to rinse off, then moved along the sides of his torso. "What were you hunting?" she asked, trying to sound indifferent about it.

Xerus rubbed at one of his horns, thinking. "Serbil at first...then a pack of ukin."

Lana paused in her washing for half a second, then continued. Serbil, she wasn't surprised about. They were like deer with several long, curved antlers. Ukin however was unexpected. They were like large scaly creatures near to raptors save for their beaks. They were one of the fastest creatures in the jungle and hard to find or kill. No wonder he'd been gone so long.

"Well, I'm glad you're safe," Lana said. "You had me worried for a moment. I thought you might have encountered a gris."

Xerus' mouth twitched. "Not this close to the city."

Lana nodded her head. She circled around to his front and took the washing block to his chest. Red stained the block and trickled down his stomach. She swallowed hard, her mouth turning dry. "I spoke to Xilya and the council while you were gone. We are to ready a team and move supplies to the ship starting tomorrow and be off in a few days." She looked up at him with a serious expression. "I don't think it would be wise to hunt tomorrow if you can help it. With everything that needs to be done."

Xerus grunted in agreement. Lana had begun to wash his stomach when he took hold of her wrist. Lana glanced up and became entrapped in his gaze.

"I didn't mean to make you worry for me, kissala," he growled softly.

Lana licked her lips and swallowed. "I know."

Xerus brought her hand up and pressed it to his chest, then cradled the back of her head with his other hand and bent his head to touch his forehead to hers.

"You swear nothing is bothering you?" Lana asked, unable to stop herself.

Xerus let out a slow breath through his nose and closed his eyes. "Nothing. Only the restlessness, and I still can't fathom why. But there is nothing that I would not tell you."

Lana believed him fully, but still, she wished she knew what he was thinking. There had to be a reason for the sudden odd behavior, but if even he couldn't explain it, then who could?

"Ah, there is one thing though," Xerus said with a grimace.

"What's that?"

Xerus lifted his head back and groaned. "I think I ate something foul."

Lana brushed a hand along the side of his face. "Like an ukin?" she said.

"Mm, maybe." His eyes turned playful as his tail brushed along the back of her thigh. "I might have caught a drednat at one point as well. They truly taste awful."

Lana grimaced and dropped her hand. "Oh, I don't need that image. I don't even want to remember those things exist. I'm still trying to erase the memory of having to catch one for you the first time because of those silly favors of yours. I'll never forget it buzzing around, spitting at me. I don't need to know you ate one."

Xerus grinned at her. "It was the most entertained I had ever been in many years, watching you chase after them."

"I'll bet."

"I miss those days."

"What? Me doing favors for you?"

"Yes." He smiled. "But more than that, just us together. No missions. Just me showing you my home and exploring it with you. Seeing your face light up when you saw something new." He took a lock of her hair in his fingers and rubbed it gently. "Watching you discover and observe as you do. Trying to analyze everything. To better understand."

"I still do that now. I haven't changed," Lana stated.

"I know. And I hope you never do."

Lana couldn't help smiling at that, even if she still felt uneasy about before. She didn't want him to change either. His behavior the past few days might be strange, but that didn't mean he wasn't himself.

"We could go back to that," Lana said, bringing her body closer to his and pressing her lips to his chest. "Once we return from all this and make sure everything is fulfilled in the haven, we could go away for a little while."

"Yes. We could."

Xerus wrapped his arm tightly around her, and for a moment, they stood there, neither moving. Eventually, he led her over to the stairs of the bath and lowered her down with him so that she sat on his lap. A few minutes of caressing and massaging, rubbing and playful biting, and Lana had her legs wrapped around his waist. He slipped into her easily and, as she arched her back and tipped her head, he moved effortlessly, gripping her thighs, tail trailing up her spine.

"I want this too. Every day. Any place," he said with a soft hiss. "My Lana."

They made love again on the stairs of the bath before moving back into the den and continuing in their bed. His body moved slowly on top of hers as if savoring every sensation, every touch. The heat of him seeped into her, engulfing her. The smooth scales along his stomach pressed against her soft flesh as did those along his thighs. The smell like coffee filled the air, and Lana breathed in his scent with a heavy breath.

At one point in their joining, Lana gazed up at his face, in hopes of meeting his eyes, and found him staring, not down at her, but straight on. His eyes, though blazing as ever, seemed fogged over, his expression twisted into a deep snarl, exposing the points of his teeth. He growled low, the vibration felt all the way down to her center. At that moment, for only just a second, the vision of her dream snapped into her mind; of his hellfire eyes filled with rage as he crouched, ready to lunge at her. Her heart fluttered, and she went still, but Xerus didn't seem to notice. He blinked with his inner lids, and his expression relaxed just as the vision was pushed aside. Lana watched him, still feeling the odd sensation of both a subtle fear and an arousing heat that filled her with every stroke.

As she stared up at him and felt her body tighten and tremble, she knew she loved him more than anything.

But something...something in him was scaring her.

When he found his release, he shuddered and hissed, the spikes and larger scales along his back standing on end. He didn't move for a long moment, and Lana did not pat his side to move him off her right away. She instead listened to his breath and tracked the beating of his heart with her hand. She observed him, looking for any odd signs, waiting to see if anything was different. Eventually, he moved off her and turned her onto her side to curl up behind her. She felt his chest rise and fall at her back as he calmed. His hand caressed the curves of her body, and for a while, they lay in silence. Lana got up once to clean off, then returned to him not long after, lying close against his body.

"I wonder what's changed since I've been gone," Lana said,

wanting to take the focus away from her anxieties about her mate and believe it was just in her head. "On Earth and its other systems. I never really wondered too much about it until now. I must have missed a lot since being gone."

"Have you missed your old home?" Xerus asked after a pause.

Lana thought about it for a moment, then said, "Some things, sure. But not enough to want to leave you and go back if that's what you're thinking."

Xerus grunted, his hand petting her hip.

"Sometimes I still wish things had ended differently," Lana said. "That my kind had listened about the dangers of what they were experimenting with. That we could have formed an alliance." She sighed, rubbing her eyes. "Things could have been better. The vrisha could have been there, maybe even kept humans from being taken by Xolis. Then this wouldn't be happening. The people of Xolis wouldn't even know we existed."

"I wish that too. Perhaps now is the time things can be fixed," Xerus said. "Between us."

Lana snorted. "I wouldn't expect my kind to be happy to see us nor grateful afterward. It's a nice dream though."

Xerus shifted behind her, bringing his leg over hers, his tail swaying lazily along the bed. "It seems there are those who think it is possible. We might not be able to convince all of the human race. But we can convince some and that is better than none. Clearly, there are those who thought it wise to free themselves from their own territories in order to explore outside their realm. Their sphere is expanding and with it, they learn."

Lana couldn't disagree with that. Still, she was wary to return and reconnect with her people. For all she knew, in the past few years they may have only made it a goal to expand their territory and resources. Though the organization Grayhart did sound promising, it might only be one small portion that cared to make contact with others in a peaceful manner. Even when she worked as a behaviorist for the military, she was considered a minority of people who cared to bring other races into human society.

"Maybe...maybe once we stop those from Xolis, we can see if it is possible," Lana said, then twisted around to look at him. "But if they so much as fire at you or one of our soldiers, I will gladly have us leave and never look back."

Xerus' mouth twitched. "It is your decision entirely. And I will not attempt to sway your mind."

Lana smiled. "You could if you liked. I value your opinion."

"I'm grateful. But in this choice, I will remain silent. It is a human matter and seeing as you are the only human with a force of vrisha at your command, I think you may determine how we make contact with your own race."

Lana knew he was right, and she hadn't fully realized how much power over such a decision she had. That she was the tie between two worlds and whether they could be connected or remain severed forever.

"I suppose they deserve another chance," Lana said. " Assuming we are successful and nothing goes wrong. We can at least try."

Xerus nuzzled and kissed the top of her head. "That is all we can do."

Lana smiled up at him again, though this time, it didn't reach her eyes. She wondered too, once they were back on mission, if Xerus would be himself again. That all the odd behavior was just a fluke—a finite reaction—and would pass in time. Maybe leaving for a moment and focusing on the task ahead would take his mind off whatever troubled him. She hoped so.

They lay together for a long while and eventually missed dinner, but Lana didn't mind at all. What time they had alone now, she savored; for once they set off in the next few days, they might not have the luxury of privacy. Instead of getting up, they talked in the dark until Xerus fell asleep and Lana lay awake wishing she could join him. She thought for some time about what was to come. What it would be like to see another human face again. She wasn't sure how to feel. She'd become so ingrained in vrisha society she wondered if she'd even remember how to act around her own kind. It was a funny sort of thought that didn't ease her mind in any way.

When she finally did fall asleep, she dreamed she'd been raised by wolves. She had no human speech. No human feelings or thoughts. All she wanted to do was hunt and run through the jungle alone or alongside the pack. So she did just that, catching drednats and birds alike, with no knowledge of the blood on her hands.

CHAPTER FIVE

As expected, it didn't take long to gather warriors from the haven and assemble a team that included the very best fighters, one of which Xerus had trained with back when they had been fledglings. Three were males and two were females. They were of different ages and ranks but all were within the warrior class. They had hoped to have Xerus' brothers join them as well, but as they were still away on their missions, they could not return in time to aid them. As unfortunate as that was, Lana felt confident in those Xerus had chosen.

With the five warriors plus her, Xerus, and Xilya, it was a small team to be sure, but the vrisha fought better in small packs, and they certainly had enough deadly power between them to be formidable in a fight. One vrisha alone could take on several men at once and hardly gain a scratch. Though it would be assumed the hunters would have fire-power enough to hold their own, therefore they would still need to take extra precautions. The vrisha owned few weapons, usually electing to use their own claws, teeth, and tails to destroy their enemies. However, when it was most necessary, they equipped themselves with weapons called *scyths*. They came in the form of curved double blades and were made from the spiked tails of fallen vrisha. The two female warriors—Dyrsa and Nix, who were twin sisters—kept a pair on them at all times. Just in case. They could throw them far and hit their target with great accuracy.

As for actual shooters, they had those too, though they rarely used them. The guns were slender and long, more like sniper guns than assault rifles, and shot off fiery bolts like arrows. One of the male warriors of their team named Aryus was especially good with them as he was one of few who trained with them specifically.

Once the team was gathered, they began moving supplies into her and Xerus' ship which had already been cleaned and refueled by the housekin since returning home only a few days before. It wasn't a huge ship by any means but large enough to carry the ten of them plus a few crewmen to pilot and navigate the ship as well as distribute the supplies which consisted mainly of food and water and tools for repair.

The team was also given new kelva-made clothes and scaled armor which they wore across their shoulders, stomachs, and arms. Though Lana was not fighting alongside them and merely there to give command, she too would wear her pieces of armor over a pair of kelva pants and undershirt.

Four days later, with the team together and the supplies packed into the ship, they were nearly ready for take-off, with just a few more final checks to make sure they had everything they needed and that the ship was working perfectly. Once they were sure all was good to go, they planned to leave the next morning. In that time, Xilya had transferred her tracking system into the controls of their ship as well as several coordinates and a log of all contacts she held from Xolis merged with their own database from Tryth so that they could stay in touch with their allies in case they learned of any important news within the empire. Lana found the vrisha woman to be very well-learned in Xolis culture and language as well as having a knack for mechanical engineering. At mealtime, they would sit and chat, and Xilya would talk her and Xerus' ears off about all she'd discovered and learned within the Xolis systems. Lana was, without a doubt, deeply fascinated by the advanced civilization.

"It's just too bad many in Xolis still cling to such old-world beliefs and ethics," Xilya commented as they sat together at a midday meal. "The nillium especially. All this could have been avoided if they used their scientists to create special incubators for their young. Then they might not lose so many. Unfortunately, with their strict beliefs, they refuse to use any sort of machinery or robotics to help grow and save their newborns. Which is ironic considering they use their androids, called oracles, for medical assistance including childbirth. It's all silly nonsense if you ask me," Xilya said, taking a piece of meat from a plate and eating it in one bite. "And as of recently, the males of head households have been slaughtering one another, and females have fled their homes, taking refuge in outerworld cities. For all the power and advancement they hold, they have a barbaric way of going about their problems."

"It's sad," Lana replied, picking at her food. "They may lose everything if they can't come to a solution. Do they not have a council or a group of leaders that can reasonably negotiate?"

"They did at one time. But with the fight for power, corruption and betrayal have been allowed to fester and grow amongst their decision-makers and peacekeepers. Sides have been chosen and houses destroyed while others rise up to overthrow those still standing. It's been nothing but chaos and, still, nothing has been resolved in these many cycles since the fighting all began."

"You mentioned before that your nillium friend, this one named Ryziel, was their prince was he not?" Xerus asked.

Xilya glanced over at him and bowed her head. "Yes, but he was exiled. Most of his own kind don't consider him a true ruler. Or even an equal to them. He is different from them in many ways. A rare genetic breed of nillium they merely called dark nillium. Once more, it is superstitious nonsense that drives their fear of him. But if not for that, Ryziel would most certainly be on the throne." Xilya tapped at her knee thoughtfully. "Instead he is hiding away. Most of his kin, I presume, think him dead or far gone."

"Are there not those who would still consider him to be the true heir regardless of his genetic make-up?" Xerus asked. "If they are so ingrained in their beliefs, then surely some would see he is still the rightful ruler."

Xilya grunted. "Yes, I had thought the same for a long time as well. Back when he'd gone into hiding, we had discussed the possibility, but he said if there were those who thought that way, they were overshadowed by those who did not. Therefore, the chance of him retaking the throne was extremely low." Xilya's eyes brightened as her gaze fell to Lana. "However, in the past few cycles, there have been those seeking him out. When we'd gone to Nihl to save the human women, many in the palace caught sight of him. News of it spread in the more underground networks, and some have been trying to reach him. It wasn't until recently it was decided he would respond to their calls. Now, with help from those against the nillium and their empire, Ryziel has acquired several informants, spies, and followers. They seek his leadership and a way to flee the empire for good. Whether they will be successful in this is entirely up to Ryziel. For they still have nowhere yet to call a true home. Least not within Xolis."

"Well at least we know now there are those in Xolis who would attempt to save any humans if we were to fail and the hunters brought them back," Lana said.

"Yes, if they were taken, Ryziel would be our one chance of a rescue, but I would rather not rely on him as it would become increasingly more difficult once they were within Xolis," Xilya explained. "He may have new allies, but they are still far and few compared to the rest who still bow to the nillium and their empire."

"What about those he stays with now? These Yurzans? Will they not help?" Lana asked.

Xilya shook her head. "They are a peaceful race and do not wish to be involved in unnecessary conflict. Though they are willing to house and take care of those in need, they will not fight."

"Probably smart of them," Lana said.

As the sun was beginning its descent and the moons began to rise, Lana and Xerus parted from Xilya's company and went through the final stages of preparation before tomorrow's journey. They talked to their housekin and checked the ship themselves, making sure everything was in its expected place. Lana was relieved that, in the four days leading up to their preparation, Xerus had not gone out to the jungle to hunt and had remained by her side most of the time. Though he was keeping such an urge in check, Lana couldn't help noticing every so often, especially in the early mornings and late evenings, that he seemed more distracted than usual. And more irritable.

Even as she watched him from the corner of her eye while he talked with one of the crew, she could see his gaze always looking beyond, his head turned toward the outer walls of their home, tail swaying like a cat's when it's irritated or ready to pounce on something. He had been more restless than ever, unable to stay in one place for long or to sit for a meal for longer than necessary, barely eating much of his food in the process. Though Lana still believed him when he said he didn't know the cause, she still knew something was affecting him. She began to wonder if it was their mission, that being gone for so long and barely being back before going away again was affecting his mental state in some way. Though she wasn't sure how to combat the issue yet, she wanted to do something for him before they left.

Having a few ideas in mind, she spoke quickly to one of the housekin, who hurried off back into the house. Once they knew everything was in order for their departure tomorrow, as the sun set and the moons hovered brightly over them, Lana said goodnight and goodbye to those she would not see in the morning, then returned to Xerus' side. Anxious to be done with the day, she was ready to return to the den and have the night to themselves. As he finished speaking with the crew, Lana tugged on his arm and led him away.

* * *

"You are up to something," Xerus said as they made their way down a set of steps toward their den.

"I don't know what you mean," Lana said with a smile. She flew down the stairs with Xerus close behind till they came to the entrance to their room and stepped around the screen, stopping just short of the center where a blanket lay. On top of it were several plates of food including *vala*, Xerus' favorite dish, which sat in a large cauldron-like basin. The spicy meat stew simmered over a small heatpad, the savory scent wafting through the room. Xerus circled the set-up, his nostrils flaring as he eyed everything, then turned his gaze back to her.

"Just a little surprise. I wanted us to enjoy our last meal here together," Lana said stepping over to one side of the blanket. "I had Xini ask the kitchen staff to make the vala and set everything up while we were checking the ship. Sorry, I didn't have the chance to cook it for you myself."

"It's no matter. It is a welcome surprise. I am grateful." Xerus bowed to her.

They sat across from each other and quickly dug into their meal. Lana filled a bowl with the stew and threw in a few finely cut vegetables that looked and tasted similar to peppers with a salty, earthy undertone. Bringing the bowl to her lips, she took careful sips and bites, tasting the heat and smoky aftertaste on her tongue. As she ate slowly, she watched Xerus carefully—noticing he passed on adding any of the vegetables and ate nothing but the meat.

Pretending she wasn't studying him, Lana placed her bowl down and smiled. "I remember when I first made this for you. I'd overcooked the meat, didn't add enough spice, and the broth was cold. It was a total disaster."

Xerus let out a soft hiss of laughter. "Yes, it was. But I forced myself to enjoy every little bit of it."

Lana grinned. "A good thing Xini guided me more the second

time, or you would have been forcing yourself well beyond the first try."

"You learned and improved quickly. As with many other things."

"Had to adapt fast. Didn't want everyone thinking you'd lost your mind completely and chosen a random idiot as your queen. Not that they didn't think you'd lost your senses already."

Xerus shrugged. "Many did. I didn't care."

"Didn't you?" Lana asked, honestly curious. "I know you said it didn't bother you when you first brought me here but...I can imagine it being a little awkward...maybe even shameful." Lana reached her arm across to pick at a few steamed purple sprouts when Xerus reached out and caught her wrist.

"I never thought that. And if anyone did, it was their problem alone." He squeezed her arm gently, then released it, and Lana stared at him as she leaned back.

"Do you think...do you think it's possible for my kind and your kind to ever coexist?" Lana said after a breath. "Not just get along but to actually be like...like you and me?"

Xerus thought for a moment, then said, "Someday, I think so, yes. Though it may take some time. Not for vrisha so much as for humans to feel unafraid and safe."

"That's what I thought too," Lana said. "That's why I never considered making contact again; knowing that the only way I could would be to reconnect the vrisha with humans as well. I wanted to protect you from them, as silly as that might sound." Lana laughed. "Though I should have probably thought it the other way around."

"Probably." Xerus smiled. He took another piece of meat and ripped it through his sharp teeth. "But it was a good decision, I think. Bringing two different worlds together when they are unprepared usually ends badly. There have been many tense moments between the vrisha and outerworlds that nearly sparked wars. I imagine the same would have been for Earth. Especially after my capture." He locked eyes with hers, and his expression turned serious. "But you have given other vrisha hope that there is the possibility of a truce at the very least. And that is a start."

"You really think so?" Lana said, wide-eyed. "Because, honestly, now that we are going back and I've thought it over more after our last talk, I think...maybe if I communicate to the right people...we should attempt to re-establish contact. And if people see us fighting against the men from Xolis to protect them, then maybe they won't consider you hostile. We could work together, maybe even cohabit together on the same worlds...someday."

"I don't think it's a ridiculous idea," Xerus remarked. "You convinced me of all people. If you can do that, I think others will follow suit. As you said, 'someday.'"

"Assuming we convince them you're not the enemy, of course. Which is easier said than done when there are those still out there who'd want to do you harm. But still...if it is possible..." Lana gazed at Xerus for a long moment, then got up from her seat and crossed over the blanket to kneel beside him. She cupped his face in her hand and brushed the scales of his jaw with her fingers. Xerus closed his eyes and pressed into her hand. "If it is possible," Lana said. "To see human and vrisha united. It would be a glorious thing."

Xerus opened his lids partially to study her. "You want this for the possibility of peace between us. Not because you are...lonely, correct?"

Lana's brow furrowed. "What do you mean?"

Xerus' expression darkened. "Because I am not human. And you have been away from your kind for a long time. It hasn't made you...long to be with them again?"

Lana stroked the side of his face. "No. I might miss some things about Earth. But I wouldn't trade any of it for you."

Xerus closed his eyes again. "Good," he said. He mumbled something else, but Lana didn't quite catch it. His face twisted for a moment as if pained.

Lana frowned. "What's wrong?"

Xerus opened his eyes and stared at her with a fogged-over

expression, then blinked several times and shook his head. "Nothing. Just a headache. Let's go to bed."

Lana thought to protest at first but decided against it, letting her hand fall from his face. "You're not worried about tomorrow, are you?" she asked as she rose from the blanket and headed for their bed.

Xerus rose slowly and moved to join her. "No. You?"

Lana turned her back to peel off her clothes. Though her heart beat faster than usual, she shook her head. "No."

She felt his body press against her back, his arm wrapping across her chest. His other hand drifted down her belly, then to her hips and thighs as he buried his face in the curve of her neck. She felt his teeth prick her neck, and her body tensed though he never broke the skin.

For a brief moment, she felt a sinking feeling followed quickly by the sense of guilt. She didn't know why she felt so wary, but she blamed the feeling on the anticipation for tomorrow.

"If you're not feeling well, we don't have to..." Lana said, twisting her head away.

A low rumble vibrated against her back. His traveling hand was answer enough that he wanted her then, despite whether he felt well or not. "You'll soothe me, and I will sleep deeply because of it."

He picked her up, cradling her against him, then dropped down into the bed. Lana curled into him as he lay her out. He took his pleasure in her and seemed all the better for it after, falling asleep to Lana's soft touch.

The light broke over the horizon as they entered the shipbed, bathing the area in dull pinkish light. Lana and Xerus' ship sat, ready for take-off, its dark shape absorbing the sunlight around it. A soft morning mist hugged its surface as the cool air from the night evaporated from the growing heat. All of the housekin waited outside to see them off, giving a curt bow as they passed. At the ship's entrance, Xilya and their team stood ready to depart. Each adorned their set of armor plates. The sisters, Dyrsa and Nix, kept their scyths sheathed at their hips. Aryus, their sniper, carried his shooter across his back. The two others—Gyrix and Krel—were from the same family line. Gyrix was an elder of his class, an older vrisha whose scales were faded and horns worn-down but who still held immense energy. He was also an impressive bomb maker. Krel was much younger, a spry warrior with great potential, who'd been recently given the highest rank in his age bracket. He was swift and agile and quick thinking, though still naive and spirited in his youth, he was well-trained and an extremely good fighter. Unlike Gyrix, his skin had a healthy orange sheen, and his horns, though smaller, were sleek and symmetrical.

With them also was a small crew for the ship, just four others to be exact: A group of dirra—the weakest class, who served in other ways that didn't involve fighting or guarding or tending households but who had vast insight into vrisha tech. As they bowed to her and Xerus, they boarded the ship, preparing the engines for take-off.

"A fine morning," Xilya said, greeting them.

"It is," Lana replied.

Xilya glanced over at Xerus and bowed her head. "Slept well, I hope?"

Lana looked to Xerus, who was staring off toward one of the outer walls, his tail swaying heavily. Lana turned back to Xilya and smiled. "Yes, fine, thank you. And yourself?"

"Well enough." She peered at Xerus again, then back at Lana. "The dirra say the trip should only take a couple of days. We will make for the planet where I dropped off the women as our headpoint into human territory. The world is located on the edge of their governing system, or so I was told."

"It might have expanded quite a bit since then," Lana said.

"Your return must bring many emotions."

Lana looked over at the ship and nodded. "Yes. I'm still not sure if I'm excited or terrified."

"Naturally." Xilya glanced behind her once more and said in a quieter tone, "And your predomis, how does he feel?"

Lana didn't look over her shoulder, unsure exactly how to answer. Though the night was calm and they each slept as well as could be expected (save for the vivid, chaotic dreams that plagued her once more), come morning, Lana could tell Xerus was acting off. He was distant, even more than before, his answers to her questions short and impersonal. He barely talked as they dressed, didn't even comment when Lana chose to adorn the horns he gave her, and was silent when they made their way up to the shipbed. Though he might not have mentioned anything, by his tension and silence, Lana knew it would be another difficult morning but chose to give him his space until his mind cleared again. As much as she would miss her home, she was anxious to be off and have the mission to distract them.

"He is...excited and terrified as much as me," Lana finally said. "There are a lot of memories, both bad and good, of our time in Earth's systems. It's a complicated return for us both."

Xilya grunted. "I imagine so."

As the ship's engines began to slowly roar to life, the housekin came up and said their farewells and good lucks. Xini came up last and placed a hand on her shoulder.

"May Veradis' bravery and Rikasha's strength guide you," she said. Lana smiled and squeezed her hand before Xini released her shoulder and started back for the house with the other housekin. As she passed by Xerus, she gave a low nod that Xerus did not return. Lana watched them disappear one by one before turning back to the others.

"I am grateful that you serve me on this mission," Lana said to the five warriors. They bowed their heads and commented how honored they were to be chosen. Krel, in his boldness, knelt and cited some flowery verses about his duty to guard his queen before getting kicked in the hide by Gyrix, who grumbled something about "silly, dramatic youths." The sisters each gave their respects and promised to destroy her enemies swiftly and without mercy which, by common vrisha etiquette, Lana accepted. Aryus came last and gave a solemn bow and nothing more. Though he was quiet and seemed standoffish even to her, Lana trusted his loyalty.

It was expected for Xerus to be by her side as the warriors gave their honors and vows, but he had remained behind her instead, watching the others closely. Though he had been the one to pick them out himself, he barely acknowledged them as they started into the ship. Lana looked at him and was about to tell him to come when she stopped.

Xerus stared at her with a sort of grimace that made her feel suddenly cold despite the heat. "Xerus?" she called to him but didn't move readily toward him. "Xerus, the ship awaits. We have to go."

He didn't respond. He tipped his head to the side, then took a step toward her. One of his armor bands slipped from his arm and hit the ground with a soft *thunk*. He didn't move to pick it up or put it back on and, with a confused frown, Lana went to grab it herself. As she picked it up off the ground and went to place it back on him, Krel suddenly appeared beside her.

"May I, Risa?" he asked, bright-eyed.

Confused at first, Lana almost shook her head but then remembered it was considered a sign of great respect for a young warrior to serve those higher-ranked than themselves, even if it was something as trivial as refixing a band. Krel, though taking his duty as a warrior a bit too seriously, clearly wanted Xerus' favor. Hesitant at first, but not wanting to deprive him of this opportunity, as small as it was, Lana handed over the band and stepped aside to allow the young vrisha to re-equip the band to Xerus' arm.

With swift fingers, Krel readjusted the band to Xerus and tightened the straps. Xerus didn't move as he did it, his eyes fixed away somewhere else. When the band was fastened tight to him, Krel took a step back and bowed his head, but Xerus didn't respond. Confused, Krel glanced her way, looking for direction. Lana had opened her mouth to tell him she was grateful for his help when the vrisha turned back to Xerus and reached out his hand, as if making sure the band was fixed properly and he hadn't done something wrong.

When he touched once more on Xerus's arm, Xerus let out a violent snarl. Baring his teeth, eyes rolling back, he lunged at the young warrior and attacked so suddenly Lana hardly had time to register what happened.

Thankfully, Krel was quick enough to respond and shot back his hand and leaped away just as Xerus snapped at him. Unfortunately, Xerus continued for him, and Krel had no choice but to back away and take an offensive stance.

"Xerus, no!" Lana called. But he acted as if he hadn't even heard her. Krel let out a nervous growl of his own before Xerus lunged for him again and swiped a hand across Krel's chest, leaving a thin cut.

The two snapped and circled each other until the commotion of the fight brought others out. The sisters started forward first but paused, uncertain what to do. Gyrix came out next and was brave enough to get between them. He growled a low warning at Xerus, who didn't so much as flinch.

"Xerus!" Lana cried again just as Xerus was about to strike at the two. He froze in his stance, breathing heavily, then lowered his arm. He backed away, shaking his head, hissing low as he turned and covered his eyes with his arm. Lana cautiously approached him, stopping a few feet away. "Xerus," she said softer, watching him nervously.

He dropped his arm and looked over at her. "Let's get going."

Before she could even say a word, he was heading toward the ship. The others watched him go, unmoving. He passed by Xilya at the entrance without a glance, and her eyes turned to Lana with great concern. They stared at each other for a long moment before Xilya went back inside.

Lana looked around at the others and saw their eyes on her, waiting.

It was the first time in all their years of missions together that Lana had the great urge to call Xerus back and tell him he had to stay behind. She was sorely tempted, though she hated the idea of going without him.

Never had he acted up toward one of his own in such a way. Even from the expressions of the others, she could see they knew how incredibly wrong that whole encounter had been. She knew they would be very cautious of him now, and the last thing she needed was mistrust amongst the team. Or worse, disloyalty and fighting.

But for a queen to go anywhere, especially a distant mission, without her predomis was unheard of. The rumors she'd come back to would be unending, and the certainty of her right as queen would be questioned. If she were strong enough, she would say to tell hell with tradition, but in that moment, she couldn't bear to leave him behind and so she made up her mind and started for the ship.

"Let's go," she commanded. Without hesitation, the team followed her.

CHAPTER SIX

Once they were outside the vrisha system, Xilya had activated her tracking program in case of any (albeit impossibly low) chance they should either encounter Xolis ships or humans on their way toward Earth's territory. She'd stuck to the callroom in case she heard anything from her friends, while the rest of the team kept to their personal quarters. The ship had a central chamber for gatherings but, with the incident before take-off, no one was in the mood to socialize. With tensions high, they remained apart save to talk to the crew. Though Xerus had calmed, Lana convinced him to take a rest in their room while she remained on deck with the crew. She doubted he would sleep but, thankfully, while flying, there wasn't much for him to do except wait and stay in his room to meditate.

Once the crew felt secure in their path, Lana left them alone and made visits to the others to make sure they had everything they needed. Though they were respectful in their answers, Lana could tell they were still on edge about Xerus. Though she wished she could tell them it was just a miss-reaction, she knew they wouldn't believe it. She had no explanation to give for his behavior, as he seemed oblivious that anything was wrong. She knew he would never lie to her, but his ignorance concerning his actions was troubling at best.

Not wanting to seem overbearing to the crew but too restless yet to return to her room, Lana headed for the callroom where she found Xilya sitting at the large u-shaped console, looking over files Lana didn't recognize. When the woman saw her enter, she bowed her head.

"How is he?" she asked as Lana sat beside her.

Lana let out a slow breath. "He's calm."

"Has this happened to him before?"

Lana shook her head. "No."

Xilya scratched at her jaw thoughtfully. "Very strange..."

Lana closed her eyes and rubbed them with her fingers. She wondered how much she should tell her. She didn't know Xilya very well still, and this was a private matter, but the only person she could talk to about it was Xini, and she was far away now. She thought it over for a moment and decided it was better to ask for any insight than to keep hidden what was no longer a secret.

"He's been acting odd ever since we left our last mission, and his behavior has gotten steadily worse since returning home," Lana confessed.

Xilya's eyes narrowed. "Odd as in acting violently?"

Lana dropped her hand from her eyes. "No, not exactly. Not like at the shipbed. That was the first time. Just acting off. Distant. Like something was distracting him." She looked over at Xilya. "He'd get irritable too but not violent. He's also had headaches." She looked around toward the door, nervously, but didn't expect Xerus to interrupt them. She leaned in and spoke a little lower regardless. "He told me he was feeling restless. That he was having urges but couldn't explain toward what. Xini said she saw him standing by the gates one night, staring off into the jungle. She said he didn't seem himself, like he didn't recognize her or saw her as some sort of threat. The first couple nights after we returned, he would go off on a hunt, but..." Lana shook her head. "He'd be gone for hours and not even realize it.

I had to...to wash the blood off him from whatever creature he tore apart."

Xilya listened very closely, her eyes locked with Lana's. She went still and very quiet as Lana spoke of Xerus' situation. When Lana was done, she glanced away and stared at the door in deep thought.

"When I was a fledgling," she said after a pause, "there was an elder within my household who some looked up to as a guardian. He was well-traveled and had won his share of battles, so he had many stories to tell. His mate was by his side for many of them as well. Their names were Slivi and Vresna. Vresna taught many of us how to fight and how to better hunt and survive on our own. He knew many things." Xilya shifted in her seat, tail curling around the end. "One day, however, when I was older but still in training, Vresna began to act differently. He began to spend more time alone, especially out hunting. He'd be gone for days, sometimes weeks. Slivi, his mate, would worry some, but she never went out looking, thinking he was just in a mood or that he missed his younger days and was trying to relive them in the jungle."

Lana listened closely, a chill running down her spine at the thought of Xerus disappearing for so long.

"When he was home, " Xilya continued, "he was much quieter. We saw him less and less. When we did see him on the rare occasion, he looked at us as if he didn't know us. Then he began to have violent outbursts." Xilya's expression darkened. "It was like he had lost himself or forgotten who he was. In the end, we never figured out what it was, but I know he left not long after and never returned."

Lana felt her heart slowly sinking to her stomach. "Like he disappeared for good?"

Xilya tapped her fingers along the console. "Yes, he just left. Slivi never spoke of it. Though we could see she was distraught. It was a strange, rare occurrence. I know little of medicine, but I could tell enough it was some kind of sickness of the mind."

Lana covered her face with her hand, then let it fall. "We had a name for something like this on Earth. But it was something that was common mostly in old folk. Years of research and advancements in medicine drove the disease away. But it couldn't be the same thing. And even if it were, there must be surgeons on Tryth who have medicine that could help."

"That I don't know. As I said, it was a very rare condition. Something that I've only witnessed once ever, and the times I've heard of it happening again are very few." Xilya gave her a regretful sort of look. "I'm sorry to have told you this. I didn't mean to cause you distress."

"I'll watch over Xerus closely, " Lana said. "If he gets worse, we will bring him back to Tryth and have him looked over."

"That would be wise. Also, understand that Vresna was up in age and likely was deteriorating. He no longer had the strength to endure and so he gave up. It could have been much worse for him in that regard, if we are even talking of the same illness. They might have similar reactions, but just know I have also seen warriors act up in similar ways when highly stressed. It could be a reaction to something."

"He would have told me if something was bothering him," Lana stated.

"Of course. But sometimes it is hard to say what is causing the problem. Even those affected may not know or understand why their bodies or subconscious reacts as it does."

Lana nodded. Yes, the same could be said for humans. It was very possible that vrisha reacted to overwhelming conflict in a similar way. Xerus had been through a lot over the years. He'd spent countless years fighting off a parasite...and destroying whole species that had been infected in order to save others. He'd seen death many times. He'd put his body through major trauma more than once for the sake of his mission. Who knew what kind of damage had been done to his mind and body in the process.

"I am grateful for your insight," Lana said, then rose from her seat. "I think I'm going to see how Xerus is doing."

"I am happy to help," Xilya replied. "I'm sorry I couldn't give better information. But perhaps..." Xilya turned back to the console.

"There certainly could be more information in the vrisha indexes. I will search more for an answer."

"I would very much appreciate it." Lana started for the door. "If you find anything, let me know right away."

"Just one more question before you go."

Lana turned. "Yes?"

"Just curious, did he ever display uncontrollable emotions in the past? Where he could not be calmed?"

Lana thought it over. She was about to tell her "no" when a memory resurfaced. One from a time in Lazris.

"When he was held prisoner by my kind. He had these moments where he would lose himself in rage."

Xilya nodded. "A reaction to a highly stressful situation. Not uncommon in the warrior class. Have him meditate, soothe his mind any way you can. When this is all said and done, I would consider making this your last mission."

Lana's eyes widened. She nodded her head as if she could agree. But in truth, she didn't know if she could convince Xerus to stop missions altogether. She would have to worry about it after.

* * *

Back in their room, Lana found Xerus sleeping. He slept more than usual, she noticed, and, though it worried her some, she did not attempt to wake him in fear of another mood swing. Instead, she sat down on the edge of their small inner bed and watched him for a long time before undressing and joining him, placing herself against his backside, one hand resting carefully on his ribcage. He did not stir at her touch; the only movement came from the slight rise and fall of his chest. He barely made a sound save the soft hiss of breath. Lana patted his side gently and just lay there next to him, letting her mind race, letting memories and "what ifs" clash and collide like angry waves in her head.

Eventually, she must have fallen asleep because she found herself in her father's house again, the radio playing static, the smell of tobacco wafting in the air. She stood alone in the living room while outside a terrible storm raged. She watched through the window as the deck flooded and the windows cracked from flying debris. The house shook, and the roof rattled as if being ripped open, but all Lana could do was stand there and watch. She woke in the dark sometime after, heart racing, stomach in knots, but she didn't leave Xerus' side even to walk around the ship to ease her mind. She thought about the story Xilya had told her and knew, if Xerus got worse, she couldn't just keep waiting and watching. She would have to make a decision that could harm years of trust between them.

CHAPTER SEVEN

Though she fell in and out of dreams, Lana eventually found some small measure of sleep before the lights brightened in the room and woke her. Blinking several times, she turned her head and reached out, only to find the other side of the bed empty.

Sitting up, she looked around and her stomach twisted once more in fear. Rising out of the bed, she dressed quickly in her kelva pants and top and exited the room. The passageways of the ship were empty, but she could hear the voices of several close by. As she entered the central chamber, she found Xerus there, talking with Gyrix and Krel. Heart leaping in her chest, she started for them only to see Krel and Gyrix bow their heads to Xerus, with Krel dipping lower than necessary. They each were calm, with no waving tails or defense postures. They talked quietly until they saw her, and Krel and Gyrix grew silent.

"Risa," they said as Lana approached. She acknowledged them enough not to be considered rude, then looked to Xerus. He looked normal. In fact, he looked much better than before. His eyes were clear and focused, his gaze direct as usual. He peered down at her with a curious and somewhat amused gaze, and Lana nearly let out a sigh of relief as his mouth widened back in a smile made just for her.

"Risa," Xerus bowed his head. "Did you sleep well?"

Lana opened her mouth and was about to say 'no' but instead said, "Well enough. Are you all right?"

"I'm fine." He tilted his head. "Are you? You seem...startled."

Lana looked at Krel and Gyrix. "Do you mind if my predomis and I talk in private?"

"Of course, Risa," Krel said. They each slipped off, leaving her and Xerus alone. Lana looked back at Xerus, studying him closely.

"You're sure you're fine?" Lana asked after a pause.

"I am well, yes."

"What were you and the others talking about?"

"Just their part in this mission. I have assigned them to build a few types of explosives in case they are needed."

"And?" Lana said.

"And what?"

"Did you...did you say anything to Krel about what happened between you two before takeoff?"

"Ah," Xerus scratched at his neck. "Yes. I explained I wasn't feeling well. They understood."

Lana frowned. "That's it?"

"They were concerned at first, but I assured them I was fine and that it was misbehavior on my part. I took the blame and said they should no longer worry about it."

Lana tilted her head at him. "And they accepted your reasoning?"

"Yes, we are on better terms now."

Lana nodded though she still watched him carefully, waiting for any signs of change and seeing none. "But you're feeling better now?"

"Yes, better. Meditation and sleep helped, I think." Xerus reached out and brought her close to him. "I did not worry you too much, did I?"

Lana knew she couldn't lie to him. After her and Xilya's discussion and how he had acted back on Tryth, she couldn't casually blow it off. "You did, actually," she confessed. "I'd never seen you act that way. You scared me."

Xerus' expression grew very serious. "Scared you?"

Lana nodded. "Xerus, I think something might be very wrong."

Xerus rubbed her back gently. "Whatever it was, I believe it has passed. I feel much more clear now."

"But what if it hasn't passed?" Lana asked. "What if it gets worse?"

Xerus didn't seem to know what to say at first, and there were few times he was ever without words. After a long moment, he said, "If I begin to feel unwell again, then I will meditate some more. But believe me when I say I am well now and here with you. My head no longer hurts, I no longer even feel restless or distracted. I feel the most calm I've felt since before returning to Tryth."

"Do you think it was something at home that was making you act that way?" Lana said, surprised.

"Maybe so." Xerus cupped her jaw in his hand and lifted her head. "But the storm has passed. You needn't be afraid."

Lana felt a small weight lift off her chest. Maybe it was true. Maybe it was something back on Tryth that had been affecting him and, now that they were away, he was himself again. She let out a slow breath and wrapped an arm around him. She rose up on her toes, and he, in turn, lowered his head and grazed his mouth to hers with a rough kiss.

"Don't scare me like that again," Lana said after they parted.

"With all my will," he replied.

"We might have to deal with the problem when we get back to Tryth."

"Then we will after, if it is still a problem."

Though relieved, Lana wondered if she should still mention to him about her and Xilya's conversation when the door to the chamber slid open, and one of the dirra swept through in a hurry.

"I don't mean to intrude," she said with a bow. "But Xilya is asking for you both. She says it is urgent."

Lana glanced up at him, and he in turn gazed down at her. Lana separated from him then turned to the crew-woman. "Then we will see her."

* * *

Back inside the callroom, Lana and Xerus found Xilya at the console as if she'd never left it in the time they had slept. As she turned to them, her eyes were bright with excitement.

"I just received word from my friends in Xolis," she said. "They have caught our signal and would like to make contact."

Lana froze in surprise, then sat down on a chair beside her. "They were able to reach us from this distance after all?"

"With a more advanced messaging system on a ship like this, yes, it is possible." Xilya navigated the call system controls until the room darkened, and a wave of orange light washed over them. The walls of the call room glowed a dull red before the light hit upon a central point in the room just in front of the console.

"Can they understand us?" Lana asked.

"I have added Xolian to the database. The translator should pick us both up. Ah, they are coming in now," Xilya said as a shadowy blur formed at the center which reshaped into the ghost of a figure. The light spread out over the room, and details began to form, bringing a separate chamber into view that melded with their own. At the center, a blue man with silver eyes, dark hair, and strange crown-like points on either side of his head came into focus before them. He wore a black uniform with silver buttons and green lining. The room he stood in was bear with bluish-gray walls and a gray marbled floor. He had his hands behind his back as he stood straight, looking very noble and proud.

"Nihl Ryziel," Xilya said in a casual tone meant for friends.

Ryziel bowed his head. "Xilya."

"How are things on Elestyl?"

"As well as can ever be."

"Good." Xilya gestured to Lana and Xerus. "These are the two whom we talked of many times before. Queen Lana and her predomis, Xerus. Lana, this is Ryziel, nillium exile."

Lana rose from her seat and moved closer to the center point where Ryziel's image stood. Xerus came around to stand beside her.

Ryziel's eyes flickered over them, and he bowed. "It's an honor to finally meet you both."

"You as well," Lana said before glancing over to Xerus, who merely studied the nillium male with curiosity.

"We are on our way to the human territory as we speak," Xilya stated. "Have you heard anything more from Xolis?"

"Only that the ships they sent are still out searching. From information sent by my informants inside Vesra's stronghold, they are using powerful trackers able to scan incredible distances. It won't be long before they catch on to some trace the closer they get. Nar is keeping me updated on any other ships leaving or any heavy weaponry being forged. No signs so far, which is good."

"So Nihl is still worrying about its own problems," Xilya responded.

"Yes. Xolis is still in chaos since...since the death of the prince." Ryziel's expression darkened. "The nillium aren't focused too heavily on the humans at the moment though some certainly know about the hunters who are searching and are keeping a close eye. Many think if the humans come, it could be a leg up in taking power; the crime lord Vesra being one of them. He is determined to take advantage of the power struggle and knows having humans could be his one step to taking control of the nillium. Which could be disastrous for all."

"Which is why we are going to try to head them off," Xilya said.

"Good luck. They will be heavily armed. And a few are lethal killers."

Xilya snorted, and Xerus huffed beside her.

"We aren't worried," Xilya said. "They will witness what a real threat looks like and will go running with their tails between their legs. If they have any."

"I trust your capabilities." Ryziel smirked. The sound of a door slid open somewhere in his room followed by the soft shuffling of several steps.

"I came as soon as I could. Are you speaking with them now?" A shadow of a person walked into the light's view and slowly came into detail. Lana let out a soft gasp as the image of a woman—a human woman—stood before her. She wore a dark blue dress and had golden-red hair tied in an intricate knot on her head. Her bright eyes grew bigger as she stared back at Lana, and she let out a soft cry. "Oh my god, it's really you."

Before Lana could respond, Xilya greeted the woman and said, "This is Aly. Ryziel's human mate."

"Xilya, wow, you really did it." Aly smiled at Lana. "It's so amazing to finally meet you in person."

Shocked, Lana wasn't sure what to say. She hadn't seen her kind in so long that it actually felt bizarre to see one before her now. It was like seeing some past image of herself that she barely recognized.

Aly's smile faded a little when Lana didn't respond. Not wanting to seem off-putting, Lana licked her lips, swallowed, and said, "It's nice to meet you."

Aly took Ryziel's arm. "I've been wanting to meet you since...since I started with Grayhart really. I never thought this day would happen."

"So...it's true then," Lana started slowly. "What Xilya said...you and others were taken to Xolis."

Aly's smile turned sad. "Yes." She explained about Grayhart and their mission to explore advanced civilizations and how she and her team ended up in Xolis and what followed after. "Then Ryziel brought me here," she said. "We hid for a while until others started contacting us. Then we started to act, trying to follow the workings of those hunting humans for Xolis. Waiting in hopes that we would hear back from Xilya and eventually from you."

"You never tried to contact Earth?" Lana asked.

"We did but..." Aly frowned. "It's been difficult. My team was told to warn them of hunters from Xolis, and I'm confident they've told everyone they could, but lately Earth and its territories have been silent about their plans. I'm not sure they fully trust us. But there are rumors they've been gearing up for a possible confrontation with the Xolis ships."

"So they have been preparing?"

"We think so, but they don't know where or when the ships might strike. The territories are vast, as you know," Aly said.

"Which is why we hope to find them first," Xilya replied.

"It's good that you do," Aly said. "As far as humans have come, I don't think our military is as ready as we think. Xolis' is far more advanced."

"We will...do our best to keep them from others," Lana said.

Aly had opened her mouth to respond when something tugged at her skirt. She looked down and grinned. "Come say hi, Tarzil."

Out from her skirts, a pale bluish child poked his head out. Though the small boy had features just like Ryziel's, his eyes were like his mother's—a bright blue-green.

"Is that...yours?" Lana asked, stunned.

Aly smiled up at her. "My son, yes." She gently coaxed the boy between her and her father. Ryziel squeezed the boy's shoulder, looking down at him with pride.

Lana felt the sudden need to sit. She glanced up at Xerus, who met her stare as she sat at one of the chairs by the console. It was one thing to hear the story from Xilya about humans giving birth to another kind's offspring, but actually seeing it was completely different. Because for all her years of scientific research, the data told her that it was impossible, yet here was proof right before her.

"There is another here. Sarah," Aly continued. "She has a son as well, a little older than mine. He wasn't feeling well, so they are sleeping."

Lana nodded her head as if she understood. As if alien hybrids were just a thing one expected. "And your boy, he looks to be five or six," Lana heard herself say. "But you'd only fled Xolis a little over a year ago..."

"They grow at a much faster rate than humans," Aly answered.

"Ah...that is...honestly quite fascinating," Lana said. "I would be interested to see any data on his birth and growth."

"I would love to give you more detail on that when we see each other in person."

Lana's eyes widened. "You're going to come to Tryth?"

Aly and Ryziel locked eyes, and Ryziel took her hand and squeezed it gently. Aly looked back at her and said, "Well, we aren't sure yet but...eventually we would like to leave Elestyl. As good as the Yurzans have been to us, we want to find our own home." Aly shrugged. "And with the people starting to fight Xolis' rule and looking to get out of the empire, it would be nice to find a permanent place for all of us, as far from Xolis as we can get. A place where everyone is safe. Sarah and I hoped to see a few familiar human faces too. If possible. It might be a pipedream, but with Grayhart and many Xolians being open-minded to other races, it would be nice to find a place where all are welcome. There are so many planets in this universe, there has to be one...or even a few in the same solar system..."

Lana blinked and looked to Xerus then back to Aly. "It's not a bad dream. I don't think Tryth is the right planet but...somewhere."

Aly nodded and smiled. "Somewhere. But even if it's not Tryth or Earth or one of its many planets. I hope we can meet someday."

Lana looked down at the child, then back at Aly and smiled. "I would like that too."

A light from the console blinked on and off, followed by a low ping. Xilya turned to the terminal and checked a map. Her eyes widened.

"We have to let you go. Something has come up," Xilya said. "We will talk again soon."

"Of course. Until next time," Aly said. She waved goodbye, and Ryziel bowed his head before the light at the center went dark and their images disappeared.

"We have a problem." Xilya brought up the map to the center

point of the room where, from a vast number of stars, one star, in particular, blinked bright red. "My tracker is getting a reading from a planet in this system." She pointed. "It says it's human."

Lana looked at the red dot and frowned. "That's nowhere near Earth's territories."

Xerus also studied the spot curiously. "A lone human. Stranded perhaps?"

"I think not, " Xilya said. "The tracker is also picking up traces of Ionx. Looks like a hunter might have found their mark."

Lana and Xerus glanced at each other, then Xerus dipped his head toward Xilya. "Then we will make a stop and prepare to engage."

CHAPTER EIGHT

The planet was surprisingly lush with life. Save for the massive volcanoes and molten rock, the world was a jungle and sea teeming with all kinds of species of fish, bird, and mammal. If Lana weren't on such an important mission, she would have taken several days if not weeks to collect data on the world and study the various specimens in their habitat. Unfortunately, there was no time, and the draw to find the hunter and the human (or humans) were a larger priority that stole her focus from anything else.

Once touching ground, they expected and prepared for the possibility that the hunter would have their own security system and that he or she would know of their arrival. Locking on to the hunter's ship, they landed as close to it as possible, drawing up their shields in case of an immediate attack. Lana stayed onboard, watching closely to the drone feeds, or "skyeyes" as vrisha called them, while Xerus and their team exited the ship. They didn't need to all go out there. Even one was enough to take on one hunter. Instead, Gyrix and Krel guarded the perimeter of the ship, Aryus took up a position from above to keep an eye out, and the sisters followed Xerus to the hunter's ship close by.

The ship was a dark, hard-edged looking design similar to the vrisha's, but Xilya was absolutely certain it was a Xolis-made ship. When they checked it, they found it empty but not, from what they could tell, broken or run-down which was puzzling. Why would they come out to this planet with no known civilization to make a stop if they were not in need of repairs?

"They may be trying to hide," Xilya said as an answer. "Either they are waiting on their master's orders, or they are looking to refuel before returning to Xolis. Whatever the cause, they can't be far."

"But why take the humans with them into the jungle?" Lana asked. "Why not leave them on the ship tied up or caged or something?"

"In case of people like us coming along and stealing their cargo." Xilya tipped her head in a shrug. "Otherwise, it's hard to say."

Lana watched as Xerus and the sisters checked around the hunter's ship, tracking footprints on the ground and any evidence of a struggle or of someone fleeing into the jungle. After careful observation, they concluded there was only one human and that they had followed the hunter into the jungle. After some debate, it was assumed they were coerced to go into the wilds for whatever reason.

The sisters had begun to approach the forest edge when Xerus stopped them.

"I'll go," he said as his eyes drifted over the dark jungle. He lifted his head and smelled the air, his tail beginning to weave behind him.

Lana shifted nervously in her seat. "Maybe he shouldn't go alone," she said to Xilya beside her.

Xilya gave her a curious look. "Why? He is more than capable."

Lana knew that more than anyone. Still, something bothered her in the way he paced as if ready to charge into the underbrush.

"It looks like he might have picked up a scent," Xilya commented.

The sisters backed away but stayed close to the perimeter of the ship as Xerus found an opening and slipped inside.

It took a moment for one of the skyeyes to find him as it followed from above. He moved swiftly and silently through the forest, his body low to the ground. The way he moved reminded Lana of a jungle cat hunting its prey. Her heart fluttered at the sight, but she remained quiet and still as she watched, confident he was close. Even if the hunter had a weapon, she didn't think they would be able to use it in time before Xerus attacked. And if there was a trap, they would immediately respond.

The jungle abruptly ended at a beach. Before Xerus burst out from between two thick trees, he halted and scanned the coast. Not far off to the north, they could see someone sitting on a set of rocks. As Xerus moved closer, they could see it was a human woman. She sat alone, wearing nothing but undergarments, her hair dripping. She had clearly just come from a swim.

Lana frowned in confusion at the sight of her. The woman didn't seem to be in any distress. She was in fact sitting calmly, drying herself in the sun.

Maybe it was a trap after all. "Something isn't right," Lana said.

Xerus seemed to think the scene odd as well, for he hesitated in his approach. Then, slowly, he began to sneak up behind her.

"No need for that," Xilya said. "He's going to scare her if she sees him."

"He's just being cautious," Lana explained, though she grew tense as she watched, her heart beginning to pound.

"Why not call out to make himself known instead? What does he plan to do when he gets to—oh."

Xerus was only a few feet away when the girl turned her head and saw him. She let out a small scream and scrambled off the rocks. As she tried to stand, she stumbled and fell back, sand kicking up around her.

As she crawled back, Xerus went very still. Lana expected him to say something, even if the woman couldn't understand him, or to try to convince her he meant no harm. Instead, to Lana's sudden horror, he bared his teeth, letting out a deep hiss.

"What in Varadis' name is he doing?" Xilya started.

Lana rose from her seat, eyes wide as she watched Xerus follow the woman slowly, crouching low as if he were about to strike.

A vision of Xerus leaping at her from within the red room pushed its way into her mind, and Lana's heart dropped. "Get the others. Tell them to—no!"

As Xerus lunged at the woman, a shadow burst from the forest and shot toward him, blocking Xerus' reaching hand, then striking at his chest with what looked to be a sharpened blade. Xerus dodged the attack and leaped back, snarling. The shadow, which was in fact a large alien male with purplish skin, snarled back, placing the woman behind him. With his upper torso bare, Lana could see the alien had dozens of white swirls and stripes all along his body and a skull-like face fixed around a pair of large, orange eyes. His scary, intimidating looks coupled with his use of a bladed weapon told them he must be the hunter.

The hunter crouched low, not moving away from the woman as Xerus paced in front of him. The hunter had two blades in each hand now, and he looked ready to fight. Xerus was not intimated or afraid. He growled low and leaped for the hunter, who shot back. The hunter said something to the woman, and the woman scrambled to her feet, running off down the coast and toward the ships.

Lana turned out of their ship's cabin and started for the exit.

"What do you expect to do?" Xilya called out.

"I need to get the girl before we lose her. If she sees the others, she'll run, but I might be able to stop her!" Lana called back. She rushed down the hall and opened the ship doors. Bright light and warm mist hit her as she slipped out and headed toward the beach.

Gyrix and Krel met up with her, and she pointed in the direction of the coast. Seeing her fear and urgency, they didn't hesitate or ask questions and started quickly off into the jungle. The sisters followed after them as they passed. Aryus was by her side in no time as she ran through part of the jungle, cursing her slow human legs. As if guessing her frustration, he picked her up mid-stride and had them flying toward the beach. As they hit sand, he put her down, and Lana started up the coast until she saw the figure of a woman running toward them.

The woman kept looking back and slowing as if unsure whether to turn around or keep going. Then she saw them, and she froze.

She saw Aryus first and took up a defensive stance, fists at the ready as if she were fully prepared to take on the vrisha warrior without a thought. But as soon as she saw Lana not far behind him, her eyes widened, and her arms dropped. She blinked at her, dumbstruck, as Lana ran up, motioning for Aryus to back off.

"It's all right, don't be afraid," Lana said as she got closer. The woman's brow furrowed. She didn't respond, giving Lana a confused sort of look. Her dark eyes flitted over Lana's clothes and armor, and her hands turned back to fists.

Lana stopped a few feet from the woman and put up her hands. She went to speak again and realized in her thoughtlessness that she had spoken in vrishan, not English or any other common Earth tongue. Wanting to smack herself, she tried to speak again, but the woman said something first, making Lana stop. The woman looked at her for an answer, and Lana couldn't seem to respond.

"Who are you?" the woman asked again. Lana stared at her, disturbed to find that it took a lot more effort, not only to understand her but to find the right words as a reply. It had been so long since she'd heard the human tongue (even she and Aly had only spoken in their alien languages using a translator) she'd not only forgotten what it sounded like but barely remembered the words.

"I'm Dr. Lana Hart," she finally replied. At least she knew her name, for all it was worth.

The woman's eyes widened, and her mouth dropped open. "Dr. Hart...*The* Dr. Lana Hart."

Lana nodded. "Yes. Who are you?"

The woman glanced at Aryus, then back at her. "Elise Star—Stirling. Ex-military."

Lana thought over her words and said slowly, "What are you doing here?"

Elise was about to respond when someone or something roared close by. They both jumped, and Lana looked over Elise's shoulder to see Xerus still fighting against the hunter, only this time he wasn't alone. Gyrix, Krel and the twins were there, circling the hunter as well but were also keeping a wary eye on Xerus, who began to lash out at them, rage twisting his features.

"You need to go." Lana passed by her, heading toward the fight. "Head back...to the ship."

"Wait!" Elise shouted to her. "Please call them off!"

Lana stopped and turned back. "What?"

"He isn't one of the bad guys. He's with me," Elise said.

Lana found that almost hard to believe. "If he coerced you somehow—"

Elise grabbed her arm and forced Lana to look at her as Lana started to turn away. "He didn't. I'm with him, do you understand? He's my partner."

Lana looked at her like she was crazy.

Elise rolled her eyes. "My mate or whatever. Now, tell them to stop."

Lana studied her for a second longer to make sure she was serious, then gently pulled her arm away. "Come with me."

They ran back toward the fight with Aryus beside them. When they reached the group, Lana called out to the others. "Don't attack!" she cried as the vrisha began to close in on the hunter, lashing out with claws and tails which the hunter dodged if only barely. He had a few lashes on his thighs and chest, but miraculously, he was still going as if the wounds meant little. As Lana signaled to them and ordered them to stop, the group immediately backed away at her command. All except Xerus, who continued his onslaught, his anger seeming to grow the longer they fought. The hunter returned his focus to him and struck out, nearly cutting into Xerus' stomach. Xerus growled and whipped out his tail, just barely missing the hunter's neck.

"Xerus!" Lana cried out. "Xerus, stop!"

He didn't listen.

Lana moved to try and get closer but was promptly held back by Gyrix.

"I wouldn't go near, Risa," he said. "Your predomis isn't himself."

Lana had started to protest when the fighters came close enough that the sand they kicked up sprayed her body and stung her eyes, forcing her and the others to move farther back. Elise came around and got the hunter's attention. She spoke to him in a language Lana didn't understand, and the hunter in turn barked something back. Xerus' attack never slowed and neither did the hunter's. Elise continued to argue with her man even as he fought, trying, Lana hoped, to persuade him that they weren't a threat.

Something must have gotten through to the hunter because, as he leaped to one side and ducked Xerus' tail, he gave Lana a swift look and noticed Elise beside her with the others. He jumped back as far as he could from Xerus to try and gain some ground, but Xerus was on him before he could even pause. Xerus' strikes became less organized and more savage, forcing the hunter to move faster lest he lose a limb or find his guts on the ground. Lana knew something had to be done. She looked to the others and made a decision; one that it pained her to make but was, at that moment, necessary.

"Make him stop," she told them. "Whatever you have to do."

Their faces turned grim, but they understood. As the hunter threw his blade, catching Xerus' thigh, Xerus shot forward and kicked the alien down, forcing him on his back. With mouth open wide and teeth ready to sink into flesh, Xerus lunged down at the hunter, and, in turn, the hunter drew up his second blade, ready to stab Xerus' neck. Before either could make contact, Gyrix and Krel grabbed hold of Xerus and dragged him back, hooking their talons into his sides. The sisters came around the front, placing themselves between the hunter and Xerus, their teeth bared as Xerus snarled and snapped at them.

Tears stung Lana's eyes as she watched them take him down, forcing him to the ground. He struggled and writhed under them, almost breaking free several times.

Even with the two males sinking their claws in him and the females grabbing his horns and tail, it took several minutes to pin him right so that he couldn't get up. To Lana, the process felt like days and made her feel exhausted just watching. She badly wanted to go to him, to try to bring him out of whatever maddened state he was in. Once they had him pinned, she could no longer just stand there and wait. She cautiously approached and crouched down, hoping to make him come to his senses. But as she reached for him, his eyes turned up at her, and she flinched, immediately drawing back.

She hadn't seen that look on him since...

Her body turning cold, Lana rose on shaking limbs and backed away. A hand touched her shoulder, and she jumped.

"Let me put him out...so we can get him back on the ship safely," Aryus said from behind her.

Not knowing what to say, Lana merely nodded and stepped aside to let Aryus pass. As he approached, Xerus let out a deep growl. Aryus gripped Xerus' neck in one place, covering the vents at the curve of his throat. Then, with two knuckles, he swiftly brought down his other hand and clocked Xerus in the head. Xerus went out instantly, his head dropping into the sand, eyes rolling back and lids closing, body going limp.

As soon as he was out, the team let him go, turning him over so he was on his back. Kneeling in the sand, Lana took hold of his head, placing it on her lap. She whispered a few words and brushed her fingers along the side of his face, then lowered her head and kissed his mouth.

Xerus, what's happened to you? she thought, an ache growing in her chest at the sight of his sleeping form.

"We should get him to the ship quickly, Risa," said Nix. "Before he wakes up..."

Lana quickly wiped tears away, then turned her head and looked up at the vrisha female and nodded. She carefully stood up and allowed the team to take hold of him, moving as quickly as possible back to the ship. Only Aryus stayed behind with her.

Lana watched them go for a moment, then looked over at Elise and her supposed mate, who had been standing nearby. The hunter looked guarded, his arm wrapped protectively around Elise's waist. Lana approached with caution, keeping her fear and concerns at bay.

"I need to return to the ship. I ask that you don't leave until we've talked," Lana said with as much authority as she could muster. "I think we both have a lot of questions that need answers."

Elise nodded and it was enough that Lana trusted they would stay. Her thoughts turning back to Xerus, Lana quickly returned to Aryus, who waited nearby, and allowed him to lift her up once more and take her swiftly back to the ship.

CHAPTER NINE

Lana sat on the cold ground, her shoulder pressed against a grated, barred door. Peering through one of the openings, she could see beyond into the small room and to Xerus sleeping within.

The room had been meant for storage but had been quickly emptied, the items within being exchanged for Xerus' body. They told her before they'd placed him inside that he had woken briefly, only to blink up at them as if he didn't know them before falling back asleep. When Lana returned to the ship, she found him in the storage room with the door locked tight. All she could do was stand there looking at him, feeling a sickening ache growing in her chest. The others understood her need to be alone with him and so departed quickly after to give her space.

She couldn't say how long she had been sitting there staring at him, but she knew it must have been a long while because, several times, crewmen had come in to check on her. They didn't speak or ask if she needed anything, knowing if she did, she would call on them. They left her, knowing there was nothing they could do and that she needed time.

Lana knew she couldn't sit there forever, hoping just watching

Xerus would make him better. But she couldn't seem to bring herself to leave his side either, despite knowing she would eventually have to. They still had to complete the mission. She had to go on. She had to be the leader they expected even if she didn't feel it. Even if all she wanted to do was crawl into the room and lie next to her mate and hope when he woke he would recognize her and everything would be fine.

Lana wiped away another tear as it fell, her hand shaking. She took deep breaths, trying to find the calm she needed to think about what to do next. It was hard as she realized how much she needed Xerus beside her, not just as partner and predomis, but as mentor and friend. She'd never felt more alone, and she had to decide what to do now that he couldn't be beside her. Knowing she would have to finish the mission without him as he stayed locked away for his safety and the safety of the others.

Her eyes flitted over the grated metal of the door, and she wanted to throw up and weep all at once. She had decided they needed to put him somewhere safe. But as soon as she had laid eyes on him in the room, all she could see was a cage. She had locked him away. Something she never would have dreamed, never would have believed, she would ever do. Not since Lazris.

Tears slipped down her face, and she angrily wiped them away. No, it was no good letting her emotions run away with her about it now. She needed to get up and do what had to be done. When everything was over, she would leave straight for home and find Xerus a cure.

The door behind Lana slid open, and she heard the soft clicking of footsteps across the central storage level till they stopped beside her. Lana looked up and saw Xilya looking through the grated door.

"How is he?" she asked.

Lana let her gaze slip back down to her lap. "He sleeps for now. I can't say how he will be when he wakes up."

Lana caught Xilya's tail flick upward beside her. "When he does, we can administer a calming spray if..."

Lana nodded. "If he's violent again, I give permission to do so."

"It is tragic to see this happen. And at a time like this," Xilya said. "I wish we could turn back but..."

Lana nodded. "I know. We need to settle with the hunters first." Lana pressed her fingers to her eyes and breathed for a moment, then dropped her hand. "I thought about making him stay behind. When he first attacked Krel. But I couldn't bear the thought of being without him. I felt too weak to deal with the rumors. I'm already an outsider. I feared they'd think maybe it was because of me..."

Xilya crouched down beside her and made Lana look at her. "I can understand your fear. We both know it isn't your fault. When we return to Tryth, I will gladly defend you from anyone thinking otherwise."

Lana gave her a weak, sad smile. "I'd be grateful." She turned her eyes back to Xerus. "Have you learned anything else about what it might be?"

"Some findings. A few stories here and there. I must dig deeper."

Lana bowed her head. "I fear I can't do this without him. I know I have to."

"It's natural," Xilya responded. "A queen is not whole without her predomis."

"What if he doesn't come back to me?" Lana whispered, shivering. "What if he wakes up and..."

Xilya's expression darkened. "We will find a way to bring him back. I promise. And if anyone can get through to him, it is you. If you call to him, he will follow. If there is a shred of strength still in him, he will remember his oath to you as his queen. He must protect."

Lana closed her eyes, wanting to believe it with all her heart. She remembered the day of their bonding ceremony and his vow to her as her predomis. His promise to her to be her guardian in all things. And to be her voice of reason. To guard and to advise.

To betray and break one's vow was a death sentence.

She shuddered at the thought of what the other vrisha would do if they thought he had betrayed her. "We can't let anyone else know. I will command the others to keep silent until something can be done. He can't come out of here until we return to Tryth. Even if he wakes up seeming all right. We can't let him out."

Xilya gave her a sad, knowing look and bowed her head. "It must be done."

"I will tell the crew to inform me right away when he wakes up." Lana rose from her spot, and Xilya did the same. "Then we will talk."

"That would certainly be wise. If you need someone with you..."

"I'll let you know."

Xilya tilted her head at Lana as she leaned against the door and watched Xerus some more. "You should know I didn't come only to check on you," Xilya said with slight hesitation. "I know you want to be with him now...but you should be aware that the others have been growing restless to speak with the hunter and his...woman. They have been waiting outside."

Lana nodded and sighed. "We should talk to them." It took immeasurable strength to turn away from the locked room, an ache swelling in her chest as she did so. She ignored the pain and settled to follow Xilya out of the storage level and into the dark passage.

Before exiting the ship, she caught up with one of the crew, ordering them to inform her right away when Xerus woke up, then she and Xilya walked back out into the steamy jungle. The day was beginning to end, with the outside less blinding than before, now turning to a dull grayish color.

From the midpoint between the two ships, Lana's team and Elise with her hunter had drawn imaginary boundaries several feet away from each other, neither crossing but both keeping a wary eye. The vrisha paced or circled or stood watch, while the hunter sat quietly with his knees drawn up, blades resting in his hands, studying them, with Elise kneeling beside him.

When they saw her and Xilya approaching, each group seemed to relax, if only a little. Lana stopped just a few feet away, her and Elise locking eyes before she ordered the team to make a fire.

If they were to talk as a group, they needed a neutral space like the central chamber on the ship. But since she didn't expect either of the two to trust them enough yet to board her ship, they would have to work with the area around them.

The team worked quickly, digging out a pit and placing firewood, then setting the flame. As the fire grew, they each took a seat around it with Lana sitting opposite Elise and the hunter, who hadn't moved.

They watched each other without a word before Lana cleared her throat and looked at Elise. "Forgive me if my English is a little off. It's been a long time since I've used it."

Elise glanced at her partner, then nodded to Lana. "It's fine."

"It's just...very sudden and odd to see another human, and I hadn't had the time to really prepare..."

Elise smirked. "It's cool. I get it. I'm just glad you're not hissing or growling at me."

"I get seeing me like this with the vrisha is jarring."

Elise looked around at the others, then back at her. "You could say that."

"We didn't mean to frighten you. But I'm glad we could convince you to talk."

Lana could see Elise looked uncomfortable. "Honestly, it took more to convince him," she placed a hand on her mate's arm, "than me. And it was only because you told me who you were that I made the quick decision to trust you. Even when your guy was attacking mine. I was afraid at first maybe you'd turned against your own kind after the whole Lazris incident."

Lana felt a lump settle in her throat and swallowed hard. "Well I can tell you now that's not true, and I don't wish any harm."

Elise glanced at the others again and tipped her head toward them. "And these guys will do what you say, I'm guessing?"

"More or less."

Elise patted the hunter's arm, whose eyes hadn't left Lana or the vrisha around her. "Sorry, just have to be sure. We had a bad run-in with one of them. Figured they were hostile."

Lana's brow furrowed. "Who did you—"

"I'm sorry to interrupt, Risa," Xilya cut her off. "But by chance could we make use of a few translators? It might be good to have us in on the conversation."

Lana stiffened, her neck and face heating, realizing no one but her and Elise could understand each other. "Of course," she said.

Xilya took out two translators from one of her thigh pockets—two small, crescent-shaped devices that could be secured to the side of one's throat. "These are of my own making, based off Xolian tech." She tossed them to the pair. The hunter grabbed them first and said something in an odd language to which Elise replied back in the same tongue. They argued quietly at first until Elise seemingly convinced the hunter to secure the device to his neck.

Once the translators were fixed properly, taking less than a second to configure, Lana asked again, "Who did you run into?"

Elise glanced at her hunter and said, "I don't remember his name..."

"Ryxok," the hunter hissed.

Lana and her team looked at each other. She'd heard of the exiled assassin only once briefly at a council meeting. None knew where he'd gone. He'd been sentenced to death. But someone—a brother perhaps—had taken the punishment in his place, and in turn, Ryxok had been banished.

"Where did you find him? Lana asked.

"That's a long story," Elise replied.

"Tell us."

Elise let out a short laugh. "This is going to be a long night then."

"You can spare the details," Lana said.

Elise looked again to her hunter, then cleared her throat and began with, "I was tasked with my squad by the Grayhart organization to travel to a distant planet called Irosa to find one of their missing team..."

She explained to them about her mission to save this team who had disappeared in the under-levels of a vast city, run by a race called the drogin; about the gangs over-running the undercity and a crime organization known as the Red Blades taking over and spreading across the lower levels. She told of the attack that nearly killed her team and how she ended up alone with her hunter, who had been tasked to aid them in their mission. How they had fought their way through the city and of their fight to free the humans stolen by a woman named Pyra and her second in command, Ryxok.

"So this explains why Nihl Ryziel had not heard of any humans returning to Xolis," Xilya said to her. "They'd been found as feared, but they had been saved before a trade could be made." Xilya then turned a sharp eye to the hunter, who met her glare. "And your group of bounty hunters just so happened to be there to help them, hm? A group traveling in a Xolis-made ship."

Lana returned her gaze to Elise, then back to the hunter with suspicion, and Elise's eyes looked everywhere but at her.

"There...may be some things I left out," she said

"And they are?" Lana asked.

"I was one of the hunters tasked with taking back the humans to Xolis," the hunter confessed.

The team went deathly still as they each gave him a menacing glare.

"As predicted." Xilya hissed. "And with that, you can confirm my suspicions. Are you the infamous hunter Nezka I was warned of?"

The hunter's orange eyes shined in the firelight as he gave her a mean smile. "I am."

"And you went with him...willingly?" Lana asked Elise, barely able to keep her surprise.

"When I first found out, no, of course not," Elise said. "I was just like you. Ready to fight." She met Lana's eyes with an honest expression. "But he changed. He went against his boss and his mission to save us. He nearly died for us. He isn't that kind of hunter anymore."

Xilya tilted her head. "What makes you think it wasn't a ploy to some bigger scheme? Perhaps he only wishes to use you to find the human territories."

Nezka's expression darkened though his smile didn't fully fade. "I do know where they are," he said softly. "And I have no intention of telling anyone about it."

Elise rubbed at her neck, looking a little embarrassed as they stared at her accusingly. "He found me on one of the civilian worlds, and I left with him from there."

Lana rubbed at her temples. "And you've been here ever since?"

Elise nodded. "Yes. We were planning to just get as far away as we could. This was just a stop on a longer journey at first." Elise looked at the hunter, and Lana saw the admiration in her eyes. Lana knew that look, and her thoughts turned to Xerus with pained longing. Elise took Nezka's hand in hers and they knitted their fingers together. "But then we made the decision to stay for a while longer. Now with everything happening within Earth's territories, I thought it would be better to stick around and wait to see if we should go back and help."

"What's happening in Earth's territories?" Lana asked, wondering if Elise knew something they didn't.

Elise frowned. "You really have been away for a long time, huh? We are preparing for war, obviously. Now that Earth knows about Xolis and the hunters looking for human women."

Lana knew she shouldn't be surprised. She turned to Xilya, who gazed back at her.

"Well, at least they know and are preparing as was predicted. Though a war wouldn't be good," Xilya commented.

"It's definitely bad," said Lana.

"Why?" Elise asked. "If we can fight, we should."

"Because Xolis has technology far more advanced than anything humans could possibly think up," Xilya stated. "They will blow any Earth ship into tiny pieces. The only thing that may be sparing humans now is that the Xolis empire is currently going through its own set of problems and resources are scarce or being hoarded by those preparing for a war within their own boundaries. What I'm saying is, a war would be devastating to either side as innocent lives would pay the price, whether by mass overtaking of worlds or loss of infrastructure."

"People have been fleeing Xolis for years," Nezka said. "Perhaps it's time the empire fell."

"But there are those who can't escape it. The nillium will force those into the war or into labor to try to keep the empire alive while fighting," Xilya countered. "And there are still human lives at stake. No, we should prevent this."

A few from the team voiced their agreement while others made their own suggestions and comments. Unconsciously, Lana reached her hand out beside her, expecting to feel Xerus' arm. When she touched nothing but air, she looked over at the empty space, and a dull ache throbbed in her chest. She dropped her hand and fell silent as the others debated, her head turning back toward her ship. She knew she should be concerning herself about the threat of war and all that regarded the two territories, but, despite her efforts, her mind began to wander, and all she could think of was Xerus. She had the sudden, awful urge to say "to hell with it, let them fight, let me go home and care only for my mate," knowing it wasn't right, but she couldn't even feel guilty about it. Xerus needed her. If it wasn't for her duty as queen, she would have put Xilya in charge long ago. But as vrisha custom had it, she couldn't just hand over her leadership or her mission to someone else. To do so would strip her of her title as well as Xerus' rank. And though she told herself she didn't care about the consequences, she couldn't do such a thing to Xerus, knowing how hard he had worked for his position and to have her as queen. She couldn't take it away from him. Not without his consent.

So, better to have all the help she could get and to complete at least the bare minimum of what was needed for her mission. Yes, it wasn't very virtuous, but she couldn't care less. They were only tasked to stop the oncoming ships from Xolis with the hunters aboard before they found a human settlement. They were never told to stay and fight a war. That was an entirely different mission. And, with Xerus sick, she didn't plan to stick around to fight in it.

Lana forced herself back into the scene and listened for a second longer before saying, "We are attempting to stop more Xolis hunters from taking humans. Will you join us or not?"

The others grew silent as they looked at the pair, waiting.

Elise locked eyes with Nezka. She whispered something to him, and he, in turn, brushed his knuckles across her cheek in a lover's caress. He tapped at his ear and whispered something back, and Elise smiled, taking hold of his hand and kissing it before turning back to Lana.

"Yes, we will join you," she said. "Nezka knows a lot about Xolis and those hunters who are still searching. And he's a brilliant fighter. Unmatched by anyone."

Krel snorted. "He looked matched from what I saw earlier. If it weren't for our queen's command..."

Nezka's eyes drew over to him with both a challenging and amused expression. "I wasn't worried. Just a little off guard."

The others scoffed at his arrogance.

"You would have been torn to shreds, hunter," said Nix.

"You barely took on just one of us," said Dyrsa.

Nezka's eyes narrowed, and his smile widened. "I've taken on one of you before and succeeded."

Gyrix's tail flicked with annoyance. "Ryxok was no true warrior. He probably fled like a trembling *mimni* with his tail between his legs."

"No, he fought well, actually. I just couldn't get the last blow before a building collapsed on him."

The others seemed to think that over and were satisfied that was one—though rare—way to kill a vrisha.

"You can fight to prove yourself later," Xilya said. She looked to Lana, who nodded her head.

"All right." Lana rose up, indicating they were done talking. She needed no more convincing and, though the others seemed cautious of the hunter, they showed they were willing to cooperate, if barely. Though it was still odd to see a human with what should be their enemy, Lana didn't think Elise was betraying her own kind. She seemed determined as the others to aid them. And, besides, Lana was not one to judge another's heart. She could see Elise not only trusted but cared about Nezka as any mate should.

"Come dawn tomorrow, we will head out once more," Lana continued. "Xilya will connect you to the ship's calling system so that we can keep in contact. Be prepared to follow us wherever that may be."

CHAPTER TEN

There wasn't much else to do for the remainder of that night save to rest and ready themselves for their flight out in the morning. Except sleeping seemed like the last thing anyone wanted to do. All were restless; some only too excited for the fight to come, others—like Lana —anxious and uncertain.

Xerus still hadn't woken from his sleep, and the one crewman who had any sort of medical expertise on the ship predicted he wouldn't wake up for some time. That the energy he had expelled in his fight with Nezka coupled with whatever strange ailment he had had caused him to slip into a sort of comatose state or, in vrisha terms, deeper sleep than normal as they were not likely to slip into anything worse, like a coma. Still, finding him in the same way as she left him put Lana into a dark mood that she was certain she wouldn't come out of until he awakened.

As her team trained outside the ship and the crew made sure everything was stable for the take-off, Lana took to wandering the passages, always ending up back in the storage level, where she'd watch Xerus for a while before slipping back into the passageways. She knew she wore her worry like a second skin but she didn't have the energy or care to hide it from the others. She knew they knew well enough that she feared for her predomis, but they also knew there was little they could do until they were home again.

When the team eventually returned to their rooms, Lana still continued to wander, checking in on the deck, making sure all was well. By the planet's rotation, the nights were shorter which meant she had little time for rest. When she finally forced herself to return to her and Xerus' room, she tried to close her eyes, but all she did was toss and turn. Frustrated, she made for the supply level, dragged out a spare groundmat, and placed it next to Xerus' door.

She laid out as close as she could, facing so that she could see just enough through one of the grated openings. Xerus faced away from her, not waking to her presence. Though his tail was near to the door, she tried to stick her fingers in and touch it but couldn't quite reach. She thought several times about opening the door and locking herself inside with him, and each time she had to tell herself it was a very bad idea. If he did wake and he wasn't himself still, she didn't want to imagine what might happen. Though she firmly believed he would never ever harm her purposefully, she couldn't take the risk if for some reason he got violent with her inside and she got caught in his blind rage as he attempted to escape. Conflicted as she was, she remained lying by the door, waiting, hoping any moment he'd move.

Miraculously, she did find sleep, though it was not peaceful. Falling through endless dreams and nightmares, Lana thought she'd become lost in them forever until they faded away and she found herself once again in her father's house.

Standing in his living room, the smell of tobacco stung her nose, and the radio crackled with sound nearby. Outside, the day was bright, and the ocean was sparkling, so clear and unmoving it was nothing but a mirror reflecting the sky. Lana seemed to stare out at it forever when she heard the *clink*ing and humming of someone in the kitchen. Like a sleepwalker, she turned to the noise and followed it. As she stood just outside the entrance and peered inside, she recognized the small back kitchen with a door leading out to the yard and a small window looking out at the dock where her father's boat was anchored. The green paint on the walls was chipping, and one of the bulbs was missing to the ceiling light just as she remembered. On the wall next to the door was a picture of her and her father on his boat when she was ten years old.

Familiar as it was, she didn't seem affected by the scene though she thought she ought to be. But as dreams seemed to go, it didn't feel odd for her to be there or that the place should seem lived in despite her father being gone for many years now. What was odd was seeing Xerus working at the counter beside the window, preparing fish like her father used to do after catching it that morning, while he hummed some familiar tune; as if he'd been there all along and working within the constraints of a human home meant nothing to him.

He didn't see her, or rather didn't regard her, right away, and Lana, for whatever reason, didn't feel compelled to let herself be known. Not right away. She was content for that moment to only watch as he cut the fish open and separated the meat. The salty ocean scent mingled with tobacco where a lit cigarette lay on a tray atop one of the open shelves by Xerus' head.

"It's almost time," he said. He looked up from his cutting to gaze out the window. "A good day to set out too."

Lana stood there, confused. "Where are you going?"

He didn't look back at her and continued to slice the fish into thin pieces. "You know where. We've discussed this."

Lana had to think for a moment about what exactly he was talking about. Then it dawned on her. In a dream sense, she knew it was almost exactly like the conversation she and her father had many years ago before he'd left on his final trip out to sea.

"Are you sure about going out that far? What if there's a storm? You'll be all alone, and the ocean is so big," Lana responded, just as she had that same day her father was readying himself to leave.

"I've got the radio. It won't be so bad," Xerus replied, just as her father had.

"Please don't go."

Xerus' tail weaved lazily behind him, and he huffed a small sigh. "I have to. It calls to me."

"The sea doesn't call to anyone."

"The wild does."

That part in the conversation was different, but it didn't faze her. "If you go, I won't be able to find you. You'll be lost out there."

Xerus paused in his cutting, laying the knife down on the counter. "You'll always be able to find me. You just have to go out and look."

"Is that a joke?" Lana happened to shift her eyes back to the window and saw that the ocean had vanished, and all she could see now was a vast forest beyond. She looked back at Xerus. "Let me go with you."

"You can't."

"Why?"

Xerus didn't respond for a long time.

"Why, Xerus?"

"It isn't how it's meant to be," he said in a low, almost sad, voice. Then he looked back at her. "The prey doesn't follow the predator."

For some reason that only made sense in a dream, Lana turned incredibly sad and angry all at once. Though his words made little sense, she knew enough to see she couldn't convince him to stay, just as she couldn't convince her father that she had a bad feeling about his trip.

"Won't be long now," Xerus said, looking back at the window.

Lana had a great urge to pick up the nearest plate or pan and throw it against the wall. As she did so and watched it shatter, Xerus didn't move. She did it again and again, but it didn't affect him. She begged him not to go, screamed at him, but it did nothing.

Eventually, there was nothing more to throw, but by then, the house, and Xerus with it, had faded away, and Lana felt herself coming to. Her eyes fluttered open, and she shivered from a sudden chill. When her vision came into focus and she looked over, she inhaled a quick hiss of breath as she found herself face to face with Xerus, who had rolled over in his sleep and now lay sleeping against the door. Through a grated opening, she watched him, barely moving. She blinked several times, and tears dropped on her arm and on the floor. Cautiously, she placed her hand on the door near to Xerus' face.

"Please, wake up," Lana whispered. "Please, Xerus, wake up and be all right. I need you."

He didn't respond except with a small exhale of breath that Lana took in with a shaky inhale.

The door to the supply level opened, and Lana heard the soft clicks of someone approaching.

"Risa, I'm sorry to disturb you, but you are needed at the front."

Lana wiped her face as she rolled over and saw it was one of the crewmen, a female vrisha named Sithe. By her weaving tail and unfocused gaze, Lana could see she was excited or uneasy about something.

"What's the hour?" Lana asked as she sat up slowly.

"Early. The sun rises soon."

Lana glanced back at Xerus with a frown. She didn't want to leave his side, but if there was something important enough to interrupt her rest, then she should go.

"All right. I'm coming." Lana rose up and staggered on her feet. She refused Sithe's aid, saying she was just tired, not that her shaking limbs had anything to do with her emotions.

"I've had a meal placed for you if you are hungry," Sithe said as they turned for the door.

Lana wasn't very hungry but thanked her regardless. She looked back at Xerus, silently promising she would be back soon, and exited the room.

They walked quietly through the passage until they came to the head of the ship. Inside, Lana found the rest of the crew along with Xilya. The crew—sitting on low-backed seats—worked at the controls, pressing and swiping over red panels on the large terminal showing vrisha symbols. Screens and knobs glowed red and orange against the slick black surface. Along the curved front window-pane, someone had brought up a map of the surrounding areas including several planetary systems. At one specific point on the upper-left screen, a system glowed brighter than the rest. Its light spreading outward like a ripple across the map.

"What's that?" Lana asked.

Xilya, who had been studying something on the terminal below the map, looked over. "It's a signal. An extremely large one."

Lana moved to stand beside her. "From who?"

"That's a good question, and I think you might be able to answer."

Lana arched a brow at her. "Me?"

Xilya slid her knuckles over one screen, bringing up some kind of code. "Listen to this."

When she tapped at the screen, a voice, booming, began to ring out over the front deck. They all went still and listened. Lana's heart leaped in her throat as the voice, a man's voice, spoke.

"We are here," he said in clear English. "We are here, looking for Xolis. We wish to speak...we wish to speak to those from Xolis."

"That's human," Lana said.

"I had a good feeling," Xilya said. "I don't know your language as of yet, but its tone was familiar to me. I'd heard it before from the women I returned to a human settlement and a few times from Aly."

Lana shook her head, confused. "That makes no sense. That system is outside Earth's territory. It's nowhere near any known base or human settlement."

"Correct. It's close to it, however." Xilya tilted her head. "Perhaps a few of Grayhart's people out exploring, stationed there?"

"I have no idea," Lana said honestly. "I know little about that organization. But it doesn't seem right that they would allow their people to leave Earth's boundaries now, with the threat of hunters."

"A good point," Xilya agreed.

"And why would they be asking to speak to Xolis? That can't be right."

"It is suspicious. There is another recording just sent as you arrived. Loading it now." Xilya tapped once more on the screen, and the man's voice was replaced by another. This time a woman's who, to Lana's confusion, did not speak any language she recognized. As she spoke, however, Lana saw Xilya grow very still and let out a loud hiss.

"You recognize it?" Lana asked.

"It is Xolian. She is speaking Xolian." Xilya looked at Lana, concerned. "I know that voice."

Lana's eyes widened. "Who?"

"One of the women I dropped off at a human settlement. Her name was Kate."

Lana felt a strange chill. "What is she saying?"

Xilya's expression darkened as she listened. "Similar to the man's message. She says those from Xolis must come to station eleven. That they must talk."

"Does she say what for?"

"No." Xilya's eyes narrowed. "It may be hard to notice, but I can gauge by her tone that she is frightened."

Lana stared up at the map and shook her head. "This makes no sense. They can't possibly be trying to negotiate..."

"Maybe they are. Or maybe," Xilya's eyes brightened, "they just want Xolis to find them for another reason. Regardless, I think we have a new heading."

Lana glanced back at her, shocked. "You think the Xolis ships will head there?"

"With a signal that big sending out a recording like that, yes. I do. The hunters will catch on to it if they haven't already. Thankfully, this particular system will be in the way of Earth's territories, so they will most certainly head to it first to investigate, assuming they believe it to be a human settlement."

Lana crossed her arms. It was bizarre that her people should be sending a signal out on some lone planet. It would seem smart at first to pick a planet outside their territory if their plan was to negotiate, however meeting face to face seemed too much of a risk. Especially if they had a human woman involved. And knowing what she and the others knew, the Xolians weren't looking to negotiate. Unless...

Lana turned her eyes back to the glowing system with a frown. Something didn't feel right. But whatever the people there had planned, her team had a very good sense of where the hunters would end up, which meant they wouldn't have to wait to track and find their ship.

"All right, we have a new heading," Lana said. "Inform the others. We leave at first light."

CHAPTER ELEVEN

In the little time it took to travel to the system, Lana tried to keep herself busy, planning out several scenarios with the team if they should find themselves in any sort of conflict when they landed. She talked with Elise also about the recording and where they were headed.

"I haven't heard anything about it," Elise said through the ship's call system. "I knew we were preparing ourselves for the threat but nothing about anyone trying to negotiate with Xolis or setting up a place to do so."

"And this planet, you haven't heard of anyone stationing on it or anywhere else outside Earth's domain?" Lana asked.

"No, nothing. Grayhart had pulled all of their ships from travel last I remember, when the threat of the hunters came to light. The military has been on high alert, and the government has been making sure no ships leave or travel outside known bases. All base and civilian planets have been tightly monitored for some time. It's hard to believe they would leave out those stationed on a non-registered planet outside Earth territory."

"It is odd, which is why we are going to investigate. You and

Nezka should prepare yourselves in case of any danger," Lana suggested.

"Will do."

When she'd done all she could to prepare them, Lana watched and waited as the planet came into sight. The closer they got, the more the blue planet started to resemble the homeworld she hadn't seen in many years. It looked so much like Earth, in fact, that if one didn't know better and was lost in space, they might have mistaken it for the real deal. Only when they were able to observe its landmasses could Lana tell the difference as the land was smaller than Earth's and seemingly all connected together in a chain of continents, surrounded by islands. Also, judging by its scale, it was larger than Earth by several thousand spans. It was a shocking sight to see, at least for her as the others didn't understand. But the planet left her with many questions and filled her with even more anxiety.

Her heart beat faster the closer they got, and she found herself checking on the monitors every few minutes to see if Xerus had stirred in his holdings. She had a feeling he wouldn't be up to see them land and it bothered her to know she'd have to go on without him.

Based on the signal's origin, they had a mark on station eleven's location, but they would not land right near it in case of any hostile individuals that might be inside. Instead, they would land a few miles out from their target and go in on foot.

Finding a large open field to land in, they set down with ease. Lana stared out the window to see a world that looked very familiar even though she'd never set foot on it before. Vast forests covering mountainous hills that seemed to stretch on in every direction. Far off in the distance was a large snow-capped peak and not far to the left was a clear lake with a stream. Judging by the data on the terminal, the oxygen levels were only slightly higher than what she remembered Earth's to be. And it looked naturally made. There were no signs of terraforming (such as the colors of the plants being off or smaller and less leafy or the water being slightly grayer or greener), but that did not readily mean it hadn't been terraformed. If it had been, it would have taken years if not decades judging by the abundance of life and vegetation.

"Our map reads that the station is only a span or two to the north," said Sithe.

"We won't all go in right away," Lana said, crossing her arms. She looked to her team, who stood by waiting. "Krel, Gyrix, I want you to scout ahead. Find out what you can, but be sure you aren't seen."

The pair bowed, Krel's eyes alight with excitement as they turned and exited the ship. Lana ordered the others out of the ship as well to scan the surrounding area. They would meet with Elise and Nezka who had landed not far from them, their ship using a cloaking device to keep hidden.

Instinctually, Lana turned back to the monitors as the others went to work. Xerus hadn't moved even from the landing as Lana had predicted. Still, she felt a grip of disappointment on her heart.

"He will come around," Xilya said from beside her. "In time."

"I know," Lana said, unable to turn her eyes away.

Xilya remained quiet for a long moment before saying, "I have a hunch when he does wake, he won't be wild right away. He won't like it, but he'll understand we must keep him inside. It is unfortunate but necessary."

Lana nodded but said nothing.

"It's a shame. I would have liked to see him fight. A predomis is the best warrior a vrisha can be. "

"I don't know if he will ever be able to fight again," Lana said. "If he can't control himself..."

"True." Xilya scratched her jaw thoughtfully.

"But I still have hope. Once we can talk again, we can figure it out together." Lana turned her head slowly and caught Xilya's gaze. "I think if he sees me, can feel me, he will remain himself longer."

She only caught it for a moment, a shadow passing over Xilya's eyes, her expression rigid but passive. "Maybe...but I would not risk getting too close," she said cautiously.

"He wouldn't hurt me."

"Are you sure?"

Lana frowned and turned back to the monitor. "He wouldn't hurt me," she said firmly. "He will see me, and he will come back to me."

Xilya didn't respond, and it was just as well she didn't. There was no use arguing. Lana wouldn't turn from Xerus. Not again, not ever.

Xilya bowed. "I am going to make a call to my friends in Xolis to let them know what's happened. If you have a need for me, I will be in the callroom."

Lana remained silent and rigid, trying to appear calm as Xilya left, but inside she was a raging storm of emotions she could barely control. She took a deep breath and turned back to the monitor, her hands shaking at her sides.

* * *

It took only a little over an hour for Krel and Gyrix to scout out the station and come back with a report. And what they found was no short of a surprise.

The station was, in fact, much more than one building but several by their observations. What they considered to be a town that was walled off and gated on one side. Along the wall, men with weapons walked the perimeter. Krel had taken the liberty of scaling one of the steep hillsides and climbing up a tree in order to look down into the compound. What he saw was groups of people walking in and out of different-sized buildings, all accompanied by more men with weapons. There were "energy-makers" as Krel put it and a long metal tower. The energy-makers sounded like generators and the metal tower some kind of transmitter by what Lana could guess. There were also transparent buildings, which he couldn't see inside but looked steamy within, and domed-shaped buildings with lights on their tops. Lana speculated that they were growing their food within and had a very self-sufficient setup. The armed men could only be military which meant it was likely a base. A very small one at that.

Gyrix also mentioned that there were large shooters on the tops of the wall as well, seemingly big enough to launch something into the sky. It was obvious the station was packed for any possible threat and guarded well. If they wanted any sort of answers, they would need to go in carefully. Which meant not allowing the vrisha or the hunter Nezka to be seen.

Lana had everyone gather outside the ships to make a possible plan of action.

"We don't want to start a fight, but if they see anyone who isn't human, they will likely become defensive very quickly," Lana said. "We need to show we aren't their enemy."

"We could sneak in and find the information needed," Dyrsa suggested.

"And how would you know what to look for?" Lana said. "We need answers, but they won't come in a form any of you would understand."

The team looked at her with concern, knowing what she was thinking.

"You want to go in alone?" Nix said.

"Not alone." Lana looked to Elise. "I would have a bodyguard."

Elise immediately looked over to her hunter Nezka, whose eyes narrowed.

"I could do that," she said. "But how do we know they won't fire on anyone who immediately comes walking out into their line of sight? Just because we are human doesn't mean we are on the same side. If anything, they will think it real suspicious that two women just come walking out of the forest from seemingly nowhere."

"And to add to that," Nezka said, "they may not be looking to be found by anyone save for those they called for in their message. Those from Xolis. Which, from my experience, sounds very much like a trap."

Lana's eyebrows rose. "You think they are honestly trying to trick the hunters?"

Nezka shrugged and tapped his ear. "I think it is very possible they are not looking to just talk and negotiate. Unless they are stupid enough to think such a thing possible without violence."

They very well could think it so, Lana thought. Because the idea of trapping the hunters for whatever reason sounded just as stupid and even more crazy.

"We don't know their motives yet," Lana said. "All we know is they are armed, but it could only be for defense."

"Could you guess what kind of weapons they were handling?" Elise asked Krel.

"It seemed to be a shooter of some kind," Krel replied. "They also wore black armor and gray clothing. With a purple symbol of a..." Krel looked around, trying to find the right words. "It looked like a flying creature. It had wings. And below it was three blades. Above it, three stars."

Elise frowned. "That's not regular military. That sounds like..." Elise glanced at Lana and dipped her head. "Like a private militia."

"Hired to protect the compound?" Lana asked.

"Must be," Elise said. "Seems odd though. Why would they be trying to contact Xolis?"

Lana looked beside her at Xilya, then turned back to Elise. "We need to get inside. We need to find out what their motives are while also warning them that Xolis ships are coming, and they won't stand a chance against them, and they need to cease whatever they are trying to pull off and take shelter."

"Which means we walk there and hope they don't shoot us," Elise said.

"We don't have many other options. But we can prepare ourselves. You and I walk up and everyone else will remain hidden close by. In fact, they will go on ahead and take cover and wait. Aryus is a good shot and can get up high. If any try to attack us, he can put them out quickly. Nezka can be close by as well. It won't take long for the rest to scale the walls if they have to. But if we can avoid a conflict, we should."

Elise looked over to her mate and took hold of his hand,

squeezing it lightly. They spoke again in their mysterious language before Elise turned back and nodded. "All right. But we do this how I say. And you stick close to me."

"Fine," Lana said.

"If one shot is fired, I'm going to attack and won't stop till there is no one left who can fire," Nezka said, giving Lana a serious warning glare if anything were to happen to his woman.

"I'm with him," Krel said, and the others grumbled in agreement.

"It is not common or normal to allow our queen to go into a place alone, unprotected," Gyrix said.

Lana smiled at him. "Nothing with me is normal."

"If only your predomis were here..." Krel stopped and bowed his head in apology as the others fell silent.

Lana stiffened but didn't allow herself to falter. "I wish so too. But we don't have any more time left to wait. We need to warn them now before the hunters come. I trust you all to be ready if anything should happen."

"Of course, Risa," they said, bowing their heads.

"Then we have no more time to waste." Lana rose from where she sat, and the others followed.

* * *

"Before we leave," Elise said, "we are going to need to look less like outsiders." From her hunter's ship, she had brought out several pieces of clothing. Earth clothing. What little she had brought with her when she had left with Nezka. By her account, she had stuffed a bag full of things not thinking much about what clothes matched or were necessarily needed. She gave Lana a pair of black jeans and a bluish-gray long-sleeved shirt while she wore green military-grade pants and under armor. She gave Lana a small protective armor vest to wear while she borrowed Nezka's armor chest-plates. She took one of the hunter's guns, clipped it to her belt, and hid a knife in her boot.

The others geared up as well, donning their armor and readying what weapons they chose to take. Xilya chose to stay behind and monitor the situation with the drones from a far distance.

"I want you to have this," she said before returning to the ship. "It's a Xolian communicator. They call them techbands." She slipped the band on Lana's wrist, and the screen brightened as she fixed it in place. "I have it linked to the call system on the ship so that we will be able to stay in contact. It seems Elise and her hunter have them too which is good."

Lana looked over and saw Elise and Nezka fixing each other's gear, speaking low, their faces close. Nezka cupped the back of Elise's head and nuzzled her before they kissed. Elise jerked and laughed as Nezka's other hand groped her somewhere unseen and she smacked him on the arm. They playfully fought for a moment before Nezka brought her close to him, gripping her tight and whispering something in her ear that made Elise blush. They kissed again, and Lana looked away, ashamed to feel the sting of jealousy in her gut. She looked to the ship and felt an ache in her chest, hitting like a dull nail to her heart.

Xilya placed a hand on Lana's shoulder, grabbing her attention.

"If he wakes, I will let you know," Xilya said. "I will also keep in contact with the team using one of the skyeyes. You won't be alone."

Lana gave her a smile though it didn't feel genuine. She was glad to have the team for the sake of the mission, but none could fill the loneliness she felt now without Xerus at her side.

Xilya returned to the ship, and Lana fussed with her clothing as Elise approached, looking every bit a soldier.

"Ready?" she asked.

"I think so," Lana said, straightening out her shirt and vest.

Elise laughed softly. "Been a while, huh?"

"What?"

"You haven't worn normal—er, human clothes in a long time," she said, gesturing to Lana's shirt.

Lana looked down at herself and realized how true that was. "I forgot how baggy and uncomfortable they could be..."

"Ah, well, I am a little more muscular and big-boned, so they don't fit you perfectly, but, yeah, must be kinda weird wearing them again."

Lana glanced back at her and smirked. "Honestly, I never thought I would be wearing them again. I didn't think..."

"What?"

Lana shrugged. "I didn't think I'd ever come back...to human civilization again."

Elise gave her a curious look. "Really?"

"I am a part of the vrisha. And, since most people still consider them the enemy and me likely a fugitive for going along with Xerus when I did, I didn't think I would be welcomed back."

Elise nodded, seeming to understand. She reached out and straightened Lana's vest, adjusting some of the clips. "Honestly, I did think you were a little crazy back when I heard the stories about you leaving with your guy. Now, not so much. There's something about these alien men. Can't say what it is." She looked back and gave Nezka a playful look. He returned her look with a sly grin.

Lana couldn't help smiling. "I think it's their very unique...intellect."

"Yeah, that's it."

They laughed together, and Elise gave her a friendly pat on the arm. "All right, let's do this. And hope we don't fuck it all up."

Lana agreed. As they grouped together with her team, they started for the forest, toward a wide valley where the station was located.

When they hit a small path, Elise hopped onto Nezka's back where he carried her with ease. Krel volunteered to carry Lana this time and so, scooping her up, he held her tight as they quickened the pace. They flew through the forest at a gait that neither Lana nor Elise could ever hope to keep up with on their small human legs. Though the station was some miles off, at the speed they went, they would make it there in half the time.

With the sun at its peak, the path through the forest was easy to see. They weaved through trees and climbed over hills. Krel's quick, yet jumpy stride caused Lana to shake more than she intended, but she didn't halt him or complain. With what little she could see, Lana saw no signs of other people or of any cameras or drones lurking in the trees. The station either kept no security outside the walls or such devices were well hidden. As good as the vrisha were at sneaking around, she had a feeling, if those at the station were monitoring the area, they would know someone at least was heading their way.

As they came to the end of the path that was connected to a wide road, Krel placed Lana back on the ground, and Elise dropped from Nezka's back. They paused at the edge of the road, Elise stepping beside Lana and checking her gun once more. Lana looked to the others and nodded that they could depart.

"We will be close by, ready to move should anything go awry," Gyrix said.

"Very close," Nezka said, stepping over to Elise and gripping her arm firmly. She took his arm in her other hand and squeezed it gently.

Aryus took up his gun and moved away. "I will find a place up high."

The others dispersed, leaving Lana and Elise to walk out onto the road alone. As they strolled up the gravel path, Lana could see from the corner of her eye a shadow stalking them through the forest nearby.

"So, what are we going to say, exactly, when we reach this place?" Elise asked.

Lana kept up with Elise's fast pace, her eyes focused ahead. "I'm going to tell them who I am and why I'm here."

"And just hope they believe you?"

Lana smirked at her. "You believed me when I told you."

Elise couldn't seem to argue that. "I was shocked and unprepared to think otherwise."

"So, it was good I wasn't lying."

"Right," Elise said. "But can't say what these guys will think. And, for the record, you were correct in saying some still think you a fugitive. They might believe who you are and still start shooting."

"Or worse, try to lock me up," Lana added. "Yes, I realize it's not the best plan, but it's all I have."

"At least you know the risks."

As they rounded a corner, the station gate came into sight. Immediately, the men atop the wall spotted them. Their guns went up, and Elise put an arm out to halt Lana from walking farther as her other hand went toward her gun.

"Stop right there," one of the men called out. "Identify yourselves."

Instinctively, Lana spread out her hands and raised them to show she was harmless. "I am Dr. Lana Hart. This is my...associate. Ex-soldier, Elise Stirling."

The men didn't respond save to raise their guns a little higher.

"Dr. Hart, eh?" the man who spoke looked down at them with sharp, gray eyes. His short light brown hair was neatly cut as his beard was neatly trimmed. He looked well-kept, not a speck of dirt on his armor or uniform. "I've heard that name somewhere...can't quite recall though." His eyes drew over to Elise. "Elise Stirling, however, rings a bell. Zero division, weren't you?"

"That's right," Elise called out.

"And what in all of heaven's good light are you two doing just strolling up here from out of nowhere?"

"We heard your signal," Lana replied. "We were on our way back to Earth's systems when we caught on to your message."

The man's eyebrows rose. "That right?"

"Yes, and we've come to talk about Xolis."

The men glanced at each other without moving, while their leader, from what Lana could gather, merely stared back at them.

"You've come to just talk, huh?"

"Yes."

"And I suppose those you got hiding around are here to join up in the conversation?"

Lana fell silent, and Elise shifted beside her.

"Oh, you honestly think we didn't know? Come on, two girls just strolling up all by their lonesome? I don't think so. We got readings of a ship landing nearby. So, why don't you tell us what you're really doing here?"

"I promise you, sir—"

"Call me Jameson."

"Sir...Jameson," Lana said carefully, "that I am being very honest with you. We are here to talk about Xolis. And the threat they pose."

"I see." Jameson leaned out and waved for them to come closer. Cautiously, they stepped nearer to the gate as the men kept their aim tight on them.

"Here's the thing though," Jameson said. "This is a private facility. This whole planet is under our careful eye. And that message was addressed to the Xolis folk, not to anyone else, you understand? Anyone else who comes is considered trespassing." Lana opened her mouth, and the man halted her with a hand. "And as such, you are trespassing. Trespassers are shot on sight."

Lana and Elise didn't move, and it seemed the whole forest around them went very still and quiet. Lana could imagine her team taking aim, ready to strike at any moment.

"I think it would be better for you if you didn't shoot us," she said.

"Is that because those you got hiding will respond to such an action?"

"That's correct."

Jameson nodded. "Well, that puts us in a bad predicament, doesn't it?"

"I guess so," Lana replied.

Jameson sniffed and started to walk along the wall. "To be truthful, I'd hate to take out a pair of fine females such as yourselves. But I have to protect this facility as well and do my duty to keep outsiders from knowing about us." He stopped by one of the large guns connected to the top of the wall and patted its side. "I don't want to shoot you down like dogs. But imprisonment, I'm afraid, may be your best option. Until we can figure out what you're looking for here."

"I don't think that's going to work either," Lana said.

"Wish I could say otherwise."

Lana lowered her arms and glanced at Elise before returning her gaze to Jameson. "I don't think you understand. If you try to take us or shoot us, I can guarantee my men will retaliate. We could have made our way in by force, but I chose to walk here alone with my associate in hopes you'd understand we only wish to talk."

"Threatening isn't going to help your case."

"I'm not threatening. I'm giving you a warning," Lana explained. "We don't wish to fight."

Jameson seemed to think it over. He gestured to one of his men, and they talked low for some time. The rest of the guards kept their guns aimed and ready. Eventually, Jameson turned back to them.

"Afraid it's a no-go," he said casually. "If your men don't want to stand down, we will gladly respond in kind." He patted the gun again. "Now start forward slowly. If you make a wrong move or your soldier there so much as goes for her gun, we won't hesitate to fire."

Lana didn't move, and neither did Elise.

"Did you not hear me, or did your feet stop working? Cause we can get them going again." He lifted his hand, and the men dropped their aim toward the women's feet.

Lana thought quickly, trying to work out a response. Whether she and Elise went with them or not, she knew her team would respond at any moment. "You don't want to do this."

"I think I do. Start walking. We will give you two seconds. One—"

A loud buzzer sounded, followed by a heavy click from a speaker box on the wall. "Halt, Jameson," came a voice from the speaker.

Jameson nearly rolled his eyes as he turned to the box. He put up a finger indicating to wait one moment, then pressed a button and grabbed hold of a small phone connected to the box's side. They waited as he spoke with someone unseen, tension rising in every moment. When he finished, he returned the phone to the box and turned back to them with an annoyed expression.

"Seems you're in luck today," he said grimly. "Open the gate," he ordered his men. Guns dropped and the men moved off to the side as the gate screeched open.

Lana let out a slow breath. She and Elise relaxed briefly as the station was revealed before them. From inside, a pair in labcoats—a woman and a man—came running toward them. The man, to Lana's great surprise, wasn't a human but, in fact, a gyda male, a fish-like species whose people Lana had long ago studied but hadn't seen in years.

The woman approached them first, her dark eyes wide with excitement. "I can't believe it's really you." She shook her head in disbelief, her thick curls swaying. "Dr. Hart, it is so good to meet you." She put out her hand. "I'm Dr. Siera. You can call me Bo."

Reluctantly, Lana took her hand and shook it. The woman gave her a bright grin that, for a moment, reminded Lana of her friend, Nicole. Her grin quickly disappeared when Jameson appeared and stood by the gate, watching them.

"I'm sorry you had to deal with all that," she said in a low voice. "But they have very strict measures here now."

"It's all right," Lana said. "Are you in charge here?"

"Not exactly. I'm one of the head officials of the station, but the current powers that be are inside." She gave Jameson a dirty look before fixing Lana with another smile. "You can come through, and we can talk at the center."

Lana looked to Elise. Elise glanced at Jameson with a frown, then turned her back and stepped away. She brought up the techband on her wrist and spoke softly. Lana turned to Bo, her eyes drifting over to the gyda male nearby.

"That's Abrohs," Bo said. "He's another head official and my good friend. He recognized you right away. He'd seen you once many years ago on a gyda reserve."

Abrohs tapped his chin and extended his palm in welcome. Lana did the same in turn.

Elise returned to Lana's side and leaned in close. "We're good to go," she said softly. "They'll be close, watching."

Lana knew she meant the team and Nezka. She locked eyes with Jameson, who gestured for his men to circle them.

"Only you two," he remarked. "I see one non-human thing that isn't a gyda trying to get in and I order my men to shoot. Keep your guys away, and we won't have a problem, got it?"

Lana nodded. Bo gestured for them to follow and, looking out to the forest, Lana walked with them. She felt an uneasiness as the gates closed behind them, but she didn't worry yet about being locked up or harmed. Though the soldiers were concerning, she sensed Bo was trustworthy enough and the gyda to be non-threatening. She took in the surrounding buildings, many looking like living quarters while some were clearly places for work or for socializing. People walked about, many stopping to watch them pass. There were both gyda and humans walking and talking together, mingling as she had never seen before. In the reserves and on the bases, the gyda kept to their own groups though they participated in human society. Here, the gyda society and the humans' were one and the same.

"What is this place?" Lana asked.

Bo smiled back at her. "Station Eleven is the technical term it was first given, but many are calling it New Haven. The biggest inter-species community of XL-o8. Haven't thought of a better name for the planet yet." Her smile turned into a grin that really did remind Lana of Nicole's once bright and cheery smile. "Welcome to the first ungoverned, outerworld city."

CHAPTER TWELVE

They came to the largest building in the station, a wide, circular structure with a large, metal and glass dome at its center. They walked through the foyer and through a large doorway where they entered into a wide-open space with the dome high above them. On the ground floor, Lana thought she had stepped into the past as she witnessed scientists and engineers, both gyda and human, working together alongside high-tech machines and giant monitors. There were even a couple of scibots walking around, carrying materials from one side to the other, assisting those when needed. There were plants and other creatures being studied in tanks, what she took to be those from the actual planet itself, and operating tables alongside what she could only assume were advanced medical equipment.

"This is where we do all our research," Bo explained. "The gyda, as I'm sure you remember discovering from your time studying them, have amazing medical skills. They helped to build many of our latest equipment and create new medicines."

Lana did remember some. It was why the military had sponsored so much of her research at the time. They wanted their knowledge of healing and medical expertise. Of course, she had wanted them to be more than just another tool for the military to use. It was only through compromise that her research team had been able to push for the gyda to be integrated into human society.

Though, back then, she had been proud of how close they had come even when all the gyda had were at the reserves and bases to interact with people. Now, seeing this station, she realized how much more could have been done. The gyda had never been given jobs or allowed to be a part of certain events while within Earth's territories. They were never allowed to travel to civilian worlds or experience the same things as other people. Their home world, Dornn, was all they had left of their culture but was slowly fading away. When the research teams first discovered the gyda, they found that their planet, an ocean world, was drying up. It was why the gyda were willing to make contact with them in the first place. It was sad to see the outcome as the refugees took to the base planets, but seeing them together now in New Haven filled Lana with surprising hope. It reminded her of a time years ago now when she had dreamed of seeing such a connection between other species. It had been her greatest goal to witness a perfect integration. Being with the vrisha, she'd forgotten, and for that, she felt partially ashamed.

Through her fear—much due to what happened at Lazris—she had closed off any sort of possibility that such a society was possible.

"This is...amazing," Lana said with honesty. "When did you come here? Start all this?"

"Not long after you disappeared, truthfully," Bo said. "But before we got here, the planet had only a small research station, used by an independent expedition team. Before Grayhart started, there were just those few ships willing to travel outside the boundaries, sponsored usually by some corporation or nonprofit. Government teams went out to find planets to terraform or scout them for bases, to add them to Earth's register and expand Earth's governing systems. These independent teams, however, were looking to get away from all that. To escape Earth's rule and find a new home. The expedition team of this planet wanted to do just that for XL-o8. They got together with a few other organizations and together created Project Gemini. Which is us." Bo smiled. "With a goal to make a new home for all. We saw how segregated and poorly treated the gyda were, despite the fact that they had been a part of Earth society. So, we made a plan to make a community here, where humans and gyda lived equally."

"So, you did what the government claimed they would do," Elise said from beside her. "An integrated city."

"More or less," Bo said. She walked over to a large machine Lana couldn't identify, where Abrohs took a seat at a terminal beside it. "As you can see, this small community is all we have after so many years. It's been a slow build-up. Unfortunately, when it comes to being an independent organization, you don't get any sort of help from the government. But this place is ours, and since it's outside Earth's boundaries, Earth's laws don't affect us. And they can't take it from us either. At least not yet though I'm sure they've considered trying," Bo said bitterly.

"How do you fund this place then, without Earth's help?" Lana asked.

Bo's bright expression darkened considerably. "That's the other unfortunate thing," she said in a low voice. She glanced around to where some of the armed men stood beside the entrance doors watching them. "As I mentioned, independent teams are sponsored usually by corporations. It's the same with us. Sythtec Industries gave us all the equipment and supplies we needed in exchange for access to resources from the planet. We thought it a small price to pay. They were a company that made parts for ships and robotic equipment. It was hard to refuse." She glanced at the men again, then stepped a little closer, talking quieter. "Then they started bringing in their own security team, saying they wanted to protect us, in case of threats. But once they gained access to our transmission system, we knew something wasn't right."

"They are the ones looking to contact Xolis?" Lana asked.

Bo nodded, looking around nervously. "We learned about Xolis from those we stayed in contact with on Earth. We worried about the hunters, which was when Sythtec sent more of their men. Then they made that transmission message. Told us they were going to bring the people from Xolis here to talk, get them to negotiate, have them bring others to be a part of the city..." She shook her head. "It was a bunch of bull, and we knew it, but we couldn't fight them."

"Why then?" Elise asked. "Why do they want Xolis to come here?"

"They want their tech. Their weapons," Bo whispered. "They honestly think they can fight them and win. We learned all too late they don't just make ship and robotic parts, they make weapons too. They kept that from us," she hissed. "And we are certain they are aligning now with the military—"

"Dr. Siera," came a booming voice from above. Bo jumped, and they each looked upward to see a man standing on a balcony on the second floor. He was older, with deep black eyes and slick blond-gray hair. He wore a dark uniform with the same symbol as the men surrounding him—a purple wasp with three stars above it and three blades below it on the left side of his chest. On the right, it said 'Sythtec Industries.' He looked irritated at first but slowly smiled down at them. "Won't you introduce me to your friends?" he said in a deep accent Lana couldn't place but sounded Romanian in nature. Beside him, Jameson glared down at them, his hand resting on his gun. "After all, you convinced me to let them in," the older man said. "They must be very important."

"Mr. Tabara." Bo seemed to tense as she addressed the man above them. "Yes, this is Dr. Hart and her associate. Lana, this is Mr. Tabara, an official of Sythtec."

"It is so nice to have you visit, Dr. Hart." Mr. Tabara walked toward the stairs, making his way down to their level. "I have heard of your work and your escape from Lazris. Very harrowing but extraordinary tale." With his men beside him, he approached them with a dry smile that didn't match the look in his eyes. As he stopped before them, his smile widened. "I apologize for the greeting my men gave you at the gate, but I'm afraid it is procedure. We are very protective of our little paradise here, aren't we, Bo?"

"Yes, sir," she said softly.

His smile dropped, and his eyes bore deep into Lana's. "But it is odd that you have come now. Why, may I ask, are you here?"

"We caught on to your signal," Lana said, standing her ground. "As we were already heading toward the governing systems, we thought it suspicious when we heard the transmission of a human speaking in Xolian, so we decided to investigate."

"Ah, yes, Kate. She was one of the fortunate women to escape that dreaded empire," Mr. Tabara said.

"Is she here now?"

Tabara shook his head. "Oh, no, certainly not. We merely visited her at her home on Freya and...persuaded her to make the message."

Persuaded as in threatened, no doubt, Lana thought. "A message to the Xolians to come to this planet."

"That is correct."

Lana glanced around at the other men. "You really are planning to fight them?"

Tabara gave Bo a stern look, then turned back to Lana. "Not to fight, we hope, but to negotiate."

Elise snorted. "What? By pointing your guns and saying, 'please, give us your weapons and we won't kill you?' Forget it. You wouldn't have guns and armed men stationed at every wall if you weren't expecting a fight."

"You know nothing about it," Jameson interjected. "We are here to protect. You two have no business here, and it doesn't concern you—"

"Enough, Jameson," Tabara warned. He looked back at Lana and smiled. "It is merely a precaution."

Lana frowned. "We aren't fools, and it is our concern. We were on our way to Earth's territories because we know about the ships coming from Xolis and have come to stop them. These ships are full of hunters prepared to extract all humans they find and leave nothing else standing." Lana shook her head. "You have no idea what you are up against. Their tech is beyond yours, and they will wipe you out."

Tabara's eyebrows rose as he studied her curiously. "And you think you have what it takes to defeat them?"

"Not I alone. But the team I came with can."

Tabara turned to Jameson, who nodded his head. He looked around at the others before turning back to Lana. "They are outside our walls now?"

"A precaution," Elise said smugly.

"I see." Tabara brushed a hand through his hair. "This is a very unexpected predicament. But if you are truly here to stop them..." He dropped his hand. "No. You may try, but we will not back down to just sit and watch. You can help us, or you can stay far away. It is your choice."

"You don't understand," Lana said. "None of your weapons will be good enough against them. And this isn't just one small ship but a fleet of highly skilled killers. You need to shut off the transmission before they find you, and let us deal with them somewhere far from the others."

Tabara laughed quietly and shook his head. "Oh no, no, that is not possible. The message stays. You see those suits over there?" He pointed to one wall on the far side where a set of what looked to be large mechs stood tall and silent like metal statues. "Our men use those also. They cannot be easily penetrated or damaged. That gives us our advantage. You see, we have been prepared for any sort of conflict. So, we do not worry. When they come, we will be ready."

Lana shook her head. "It won't be enough. And if they get past your defenses, they will enter the station. You put these people in danger."

Tabara said nothing, but by the expressions of the other men, Lana knew enough to see that wasn't an issue to them.

"You risk their lives for some alien tech."

"There may be casualties. It is unavoidable and unfortunate," Tabara replied. "But for such tech, any deaths will not be in vain.

And assuming such a fight happens, would it not be the spark Earth's military needs to take revenge? And with Xolis' own tech, we would be equal in such a war."

Lana looked at Bo with shock. Bo gazed back at her sadly. "We have shelters. We can bunker down." She looked at Tabara bitterly. "Though our own equipment won't be spared..."

"It can be easily replaced," he countered. "Possibly with even more advanced tools. Once the Xolis ships are searched..."

Elise let out a noise much like an angry growl. "You idiot, there won't be a search! Even if you do somehow kill a bunch of them, they will mow down more of you, and there will be no one left. They will take the station and these people. They may even take some of you!" She waved her hand at Jameson whose face went a deep red. Bo looked afraid, and the others working around them stopped and gazed over with concern.

"You are misinformed," Tabara said through clenched teeth. "If you will not help us, then I'm afraid you are against us, and we cannot afford to have you in our way." He gestured to his men, and they responded by circling Lana and Elise, a pair taking hold of their arms. Elise shrugged one off and elbowed him in the stomach.

"Stop!" Lana said.

"Take them out of the station," Tabara ordered.

"Sir, wouldn't it be better to keep them?" Jameson asked.

"And create more conflict with their people? I think not. Our business is with Xolis, no one else."

"But we could use them," Jameson said, taking hold of Lana's free arm in a tight grip. "Maybe we can prevent a fight after all. Just trade these two for some tech..."

Lana glared at him, dumbfounded. Beside her, Elise was struck silent. Then she burst out laughing.

"I'm sorry, but you are crazy," she said through breaths. "If your brains were as big as your egos, maybe you'd actually have a logical thought."

Jameson started to laugh, then socked Elise in the stomach with his free hand, making her drop to the ground. Lana cried out in surprise as Jameson jerked her to one side. Fear spread in her as Lana gazed all around, waiting to see one of her team or Nezka drop out from somewhere unseen, ready to tear the men to shreds.

"Stop this. We will go! If you hurt her or me, you'll regret it deeply," Lana warned.

Elise had stood back up and looked ready to clock Jameson in the face when her techband went off. Nezka's voice, angry and on edge, confirmed he was ready to come to her aid, but Elise quickly told him to stand down. Lana was searching above, wondering where he hid, when Jameson began to pull at her again.

"You are making a mistake," Lana said, struggling. She looked to Bo and the other researchers whose expressions were distraught. "When the hunters come, we are going to fight them. But we can't guarantee we can protect you all."

"There will be no need, Dr. Hart," Tabara replied. "Understand, however, if you get in our way, my men will be forced to take your people out as well."

Elise cursed at him, and Lana told her not to fight them. The men tried to lead them to the exit as Lana's techband went off.

"Lana," came Xilya's voice. "Can you hear me?"

Lana tore her arm away from another man who tried to grab at her. "Yes, I'm here."

"What are you saying?" Jameson snapped, giving her a confused look as she spoke in vrishan.

"The tracker has found them," Xilya said. "They are here."

Lana tried to stop, but Jameson twisted her around to face him and tried to grab for her band.

"Wait!" Lana cried.

"If you're trying to plan some attack against us, it won't work," Jameson growled.

"It's not! It's one of my team on the ship." She tried to pull away from him, but he wouldn't let her go.

"Get off her," Elise snapped. She mumbled another curse as a man shoved her, and she retaliated by grabbing hold of his wrist and snapping it back. The man barked in pain as she kicked another away, then quickly unclipped her gun and aimed it at Jameson.

The men brought up their own guns and aimed them at her.

"No, don't," Lana said. She looked at Jameson. "They are here. They are coming."

Jameson stared down at her with an angry glare. "Why should we believe you?"

One of the gyda researchers—a female—came running up, looking at Bo. "A reading," she said between clicks, her gills trembling. "Several ships approaching."

Bo looked at Mr. Tabara, wide-eyed and speechless. Tabara turned to his men and nodded. "Ready yourselves. It's time."

Without hesitation, the men with their guns aimed at Elise dropped them and dispersed, some going for the mech suits, others exiting the building.

"What about these two?" Jameson asked, shaking Lana's arm.

"Forget them now. Lead them to the gate, and get yourself on the wall." Tabara started back up the stairs. "Our mission is more important." He stopped for a moment to give them one last glance and said, "Remember, do not get in our way."

He left them, returning to somewhere unseen from the floor above. Jameson brought Lana closer to him to shield himself from Elise's aim. "I'm not letting her go till we are at the gate, so you either come or you don't."

Lana locked eyes with Elise and nodded. "It's all right, let's just leave."

Elise dropped her gun reluctantly. "Fine, let's go."

As Jameson started to lead Lana out of the building with Elise, Lana looked over one last time to Bo. "Get to safety," she called out. "Hide if you can."

Bo nodded and turned away, ordering the others to stop their work and follow her.

Outside, a siren began to wail. People ran in every direction—the residents of the station into buildings and the soldiers toward the walls. Jameson walked them to the gate but stopped just before reaching it. He looked around, then led them toward a set of stairs along the wall instead.

"Where are you taking us?" Elise said. "Hey!" She brought up her gun once more. "Enough of this! Let her go. We are leaving like your boss ordered."

Jameson stopped and turned back. "I ain't gonna let you just walk out of here when you and your team are a threat to our mission."

"Like hell," Elise said.

"Wait, Elise." Lana put up her hand, then tugged herself away from Jameson to face him. "You can't stop us even if you keep us. Even without my command, my team is ordered to take out the hunters. And if you fire at them, they will defend themselves. Do you want to see what you're dealing with? Then we will show you. Elise, call in Nezka and the team." She turned and moved up the stairs on her own, assuming the others followed. When she made it to the top, she looked over the forest and saw an opening to one side. On the east wall of the station was a valley a few hundred meters away, wide and open with several fallen trees and large rocks. "Tell the team to move into that field in our line of sight," she ordered Elise.

Jameson gestured to the men along the wall to watch and have their guns ready. Elise repeated her command softly into her band, and they waited.

A few minutes later, Krel came treading out of the forest followed by the sisters, Gyrix, then Aryus and, lastly, Nezka. They looked up toward them, and Lana put up her hand. Jameson cursed beside her, and his men glanced toward him nervously, a few even taking a step back.

"Do you know what those are?" Lana said. "Those are the vrisha. And the other is an ex-hunter. Just one of them could take out all of your men on this wall if they chose to. My mate, if he were here, could wipe out the whole station. I've seen him take out a military base with more men than you have." Lana tugged at Jameson's arm, forcing him to look at her. His face had gone pale, and his eyes were wide with fear. "And do you know who I am to them? I am their queen. What do you think they will do if they learn you are trying to keep me? I'm sure you can imagine. So, no, Jameson, you won't be keeping us, if you value your lives. And you won't stop us." She released his arm. "The hunters are coming, and we will fight them either together or separate, it doesn't matter. The decision is yours. But you try to stop me or put your hand on me again and they," she pointed to her team, "start climbing." She got close, locking her eyes with his. "And then you won't just have the hunters to deal with. Got it?"

Jameson glared down at her, his expression twisting into a mixture of anger and confusion all at once, but he didn't touch her. Instead, he backed away, putting up his hands in surrender. "I won't stop my men from defending themselves if those aliens attack them," he said quietly.

"Fine. The same goes for us," Lana said.

"And if you order them to attack us—"

"I won't."

He pointed a finger at her and said through gritted teeth, "But if you do, you hardened bitch, I will make sure you pay." He turned from her and walked off, shouting orders to his men.

"Not bad," Elise said, coming to stand beside her. She looked out and waved toward Nezka with a grin. "I like your style. It's nice being on the more intimidating side, isn't it?"

Lana smirked at Elise despite herself.

A roar, much like a rocketship, grew louder from above. Lana and Elise glanced upward and saw the clouds part and two ships beginning their descent.

"We should go," Elise said.

Lana watched the ships growing bigger as they moved toward them, falling closer to the ground. "Tell Nezka to get the team ready. I'll have Xilya bring the ship around."

As Elise had Nezka and the others take positions, Lana brought up her own band to inform Xilya of her orders. But before she could make contact, her techband went off, and Xilya's face came into view on the screen.

"I was just calling you to have you move the ship," Lana said.

"I'm doing that as we speak. We will land as close as possible." Xilya's tail weaved like an angry cat's behind her, eyes alight with their own fire. "But that wasn't why I called. I must ask for your forgiveness."

Lana frowned at her, confused. "Forgiveness for what?"

"Xerus is awake."

Lana's heart leaped in her throat, making her almost choke. Dozens of emotions hit her all at once, first surprise and excitement, then relief and happiness, then back to confusion. "Why are you sorry for that?" she said.

"He's been awake for some time. He woke up not long after you left for the station. I didn't tell you, and I forced the others not to say anything, and for that I am sorry."

Now anger swept over her. "Why didn't you tell me?"

"He wanted to be let out, but I told him he wasn't well. I've looked into his condition and found what I believe to be the cause. It is a rare sickness of the mind, found mainly in warriors who've gone through many intense or traumatic events. It's been called many things: Wildsight, Redsight, Xiril's sickness. It makes those who have it forget themselves, warping their natures. They grow wild and savage, wanting to hunt and fight, and kill. I tried to tell him, but he wouldn't listen and didn't want to believe it. He was himself when he woke, yes, but I knew it was only a matter of time before he had another episode; one which he might not come back from. So, I ordered him to stay. I didn't tell you because I was considering putting him out again. He was trying very hard to get out, wanting to get to wherever you were, and I didn't want to spark a fight."

"Let me talk to him then," Lana said, anxious to see his face and hear his voice but also wanting to convince him that she would be back on the ship any moment and would make him understand why he had to be locked away.

"I can't," Xilya replied, her expression darkening.

"Why?"

"Because one of the crew let him out, the fool," she hissed. "He's coming to you now."

CHAPTER THIRTEEN

Lana hardly moved, her body freezing up as if under some sort of spell. The hunters' ships touched on the ground, landing near the center of the valley. Lana watched the ships open up and saw the men inside spill out, weapons already drawn, bodies shielded in dark blue armor. She watched the Sythtec soldiers ready their large guns and the mechsuits jump off the walls to land in the forest, making for the valley. She saw the hunters approaching and the soldiers coming to meet them, but as she looked at the scene, she thought nothing of them, focusing not on the fight but rather searching wildly through the trees and along the valley. Someone tugged on her arm and yelled something to her, but she barely heard them. All her thoughts went away save for the thought of Xerus flying through the forest toward them.

"Lana, we need to go. We need to get you to the ship," Elise said from beside her, trying to pull her away.

"He's down there," Lana replied, her voice sounding small and distant. "He's down there and..." Her eyes flitted around as flashes of light blinded them. Hunters and soldiers fired at one another, the hunters' guns letting off blasts of fire and lightning that scorched the earth and shattered rocks around them. The soldiers' bullets ricocheted off their armor and helmets, barely keeping them back. Those without guns swept through the fire and leaped onto the mechs, their long blades slicing through metal and piercing titanium steel. Men went down, and others took their place, but the hunters kept coming, pushing the soldiers closer to the forest edge.

An orange and red shape rushed out into the open, and Lana's heart jumped at the sight, only to see Krel leaping off a mound of rock and falling onto a pair of hunters, quickly taking them down. Following him were the sisters, who used their scyths to cut through armor with ease. From across the other end of the open field, clouds of flames and red dust blasted a group of hunters off their feet, with Gyrix swiftly moving past the explosion, a vrisha made bomb in his hand. Nezka too moved through the fighters, cutting through the Xolis men with his wicked blades. Hunters fired at them only to drop suddenly as Aryus from somewhere above took them out with his long shot.

As tough as the hunters were, even seeing the vrisha made some hesitate. But those who were brave enough rushed through the fray, attempting to make it to the walls.

Despite the soldiers' efforts, mixed with her team's attacks, there were too many Xolis men, their numbers overwhelming their own. With as many hunters being stopped in the valley and in the forest, some still slipped past and made it to the walls. The soldiers shot at them, the deafening sound making Lana's ears ring. She faltered back, with Elise shielding her, but couldn't draw her eyes away from the fight, searching desperately. Elise yelled out as one hunter began to climb the wall up to them, using metal hooks in each hand. She shot down at him, and he went falling, but another came leaping up to take his place. The soldiers stopped him before he could climb over, but it took five of them firing to do so. From far on the other end of the wall, hunters were leaping over and striking men down without a thought. Their weapons fired out at the buildings nearby, catching one on fire. The wall shook as another hunter blasted a hole below them, slamming Lana into the rail.

Blood spilled down the side of her face as her head scraped against metal. As she righted herself and wiped at her face, she glanced down at the blood now smeared on her fingers. She blinked down at the red, mind going numb. A heavy wind rose up, and a low hum vibrated in her ears. Lana looked up and saw her ship skirting over the forest nearby, then setting down near the edge of the valley.

Some lone thought finally clicked in her brain at the sight of the ship, bringing her out of her shock. She looked over and saw Elise still firing on the approaching aliens, who were now attempting to pass through the wall. Lana stumbled toward her and gripped her shoulder, halting her attack.

"The ship." Lana pointed out in the distance where the ship's top could be seen over the trees. Elise didn't need more explanation. She nodded her head and fired a few more times before gesturing to Lana to follow her.

Lana understood getting to the ship was now her biggest priority. She needed its safety, yes, but she could also use it to search for Xerus since trying to find him in the chaos of the battle while on the wall was no longer viable. The Xolis men were everywhere now, and it took everything for both her team and the Sythtec soldiers to hold them back. And if Xerus lost himself again in the midst of the fight, he too would be a threat. She went cold just thinking about what would happen if he attacked the wrong side. Desperate, she followed Elise down the stairs and off the wall. They rushed for the gate, but, as they came in sight of it, they found the door barred to them.

"Let us out!" Elise yelled to one of the soldiers stationed on the side of the wall beside the gate. The soldier looked down at them like they were crazy.

"Are you fucking mad?" he shouted down at her. "We open the gates, and we might as well let them take the city."

"There has to be another way out," Elise called back.

"No. No one gets out."

Elise growled in frustration, and Lana looked around and saw the narrow opening in the wall the hunters had made. None tried to slip through now as the soldiers had focused their guns on it. Some of the bodies lay nearby where a few hunters had gotten past but had been unable to get farther inside. Lana tapped quickly on Elise's shoulder and, when Elise looked around, Lana pointed over to it.

"There," Lana said. "We'll have to get through there."

"It's risky," Elise replied, taking a tighter hold on her gun. "We will need back up."

"Then get Nezka."

Elise did as commanded and called on Nezka to come to their aid. She took Lana's hand, and they ran toward the crumbled opening of the wall. Smoke billowed up from the fire nearby, beginning to overtake part of the wall and another small building. Lana thought about Bo and the others and hoped they were safe somewhere, preferably underground.

Once at the wall, Elise went toward the opening first, making sure no one was looking to come through the other side. Lana could see the forest beyond and the bright bursts of white and orange from gunfire along with Gyrix's bombs in the distance. Elise went through with gun raised. She looked up at the top of the wall to make sure no soldiers would mistake her for a hunter. It seemed they were distracted by movement in the forest. If any did see her, they didn't shoot. She looked over the area again to make sure it was clear, then gestured for Lana to follow. Lana, covered her mouth as she coughed a little from the smoke, parts of the forest now burning. Carefully, she stepped over the concrete and rock, taking the hand Elise offered.

As soon as her feet touched the earth, Lana was led by Elise into the forest and away from the station. Keeping down low, they weaved around blackened trees and snuck through the brush. When the trees became more spread out, they quickened their pace. Lana's heart raced as the blasts of guns and explosives rattled and banged around them. Lana could see the outlines of fights nearby and of shadows flying past trees in the distance. They came to a grassy meadow, and

Elise stopped at its edge to quickly look around. When it was clear, she tugged at Lana, and they started toward the other side.

"The ship shouldn't be too far," Elise said as they ran. "We should be able to pass through the forest as long as—"

Just before they made it back into the trees, a hunter appeared. Lana nearly slammed into Elise as she skidded to a stop. The hunter drew up its blade, then paused. Elise brought up her gun and fired. The fiery yellow arrows that shot from her gun hit the hunter's chest, forcing him back. The alien shielded with his arm, then started toward them. Elise continued to fire until the alien was on her, and she was forced to defend without it. She kicked at his chest, and he blocked with his hand. Lana kept herself far back as she watched them fight with nothing but their own fists, surprised to see Elise was holding her own against the alien. The ex-soldier smashed her fist into the hunter's neck then hit again across his covered face. As they fought, Lana looked over the meadow and around to the forest, waiting. Dread and hope both filled her at the thought that Xerus might appear from the dark woods. A part of her ached to see him, while another part of her was afraid. And she hated the feeling. She told herself she was terrified for him, not of him.

Elise swung at the hunter, aiming for his face again. This time, he caught her fist and flung her around, striking her side. He released her and she dropped, rolling on the grass. As she went to get up, he kicked at her to try and keep her down.

"No!" Lana cried. Gritting her teeth, Lana searched around and saw Elise's gun lying nearby. She went for it and grabbed it, then took aim. Before she could fire, a dark blade flew out from the trees and hit the hunter in the arm, slicing it clean off. The hunter roared as he fumbled back. Another blade flew out and sliced him in the throat, bringing him down. The blades flew back toward the forest and were each caught by Nezka, who ran out into the meadow, toward Elise. Lana saw the twin knives in his hands, dripping with dark blood. She lowered the gun and quickly started for them, making it to Elise's side just as Nezka was helping her up.

"Took you long enough," Elise grunted as she straightened.

"I'm fast, but not half-a-span-away-while-fighting-through-several-dozen-men-to-get-to-the-other-end-of-the-forest fast," Nezka replied.

"Guess you have something to improve," Elise said bluntly.

Lana's eyes widened at the remark as the two laughed. Despite the circumstances, they found a way to lighten each other's mood. It reminded Lana of her and Xerus, and, just as she was beginning to feel relief, she tensed up once more, remembering her mate was close by, and she needed to get to the ship so she could find him.

"We should go," Lana said anxiously as the two embraced and she heard Nezka whisper "Starling" in Elise's ear.

"Right," Elise said, releasing herself from Nezka and squeezing his hand. "We head for the ship. It landed near the edge of the valley in the forest a little east of here. Once we get Lana back on—"

Elise's words were cut off as a seismic blast knocked them back. Nezka caught Elise beside him while Lana fell to the ground, hitting her back against several rocks. The pain sliced up her spine and along her tailbone. With the blast came a wave of heat as a plume of fire rose up into the sky. Lana could hear the screams and shouts of men. When she shakily rose back to her feet, she could see one wall of the station, the one she and Elise had been standing on, was nothing now but smoke and flames.

Elise cursed as Nezka righted her. They watched one side of the station burn, embers and ash falling onto the trees. Lana had started toward the fire, as if she could somehow help—could somehow stop it —when Elise reached out and grabbed her arm.

"We can't do anything now," she said. She pulled Lana away, and, knowing she was right, that nothing could be done, Lana turned and followed her and Nezka back into the forest.

As the light faded from the setting sun, the forest grew dark and ominous. She could hear the crackling and splitting of wood and smell the smoke as fires grew around them, made from the hunters and their weapons. Still, they pushed on until the smoke and heat drove them closer and closer to the edge of the valley, forcing their path around the forest and alongside the open field. From there, Lana could see the hunters' ships sitting not far off and could see those who still fought out in the open, running and dodging in and out of red smoke created by Gyrix's bombs. Many men were down, bodies scattered across the landscape. Those who still lived had hunkered down in groups between large rocks or behind the now broken mechsuits. She saw those of her team, saw the sisters fighting way off in the forest at the opposite side, saw Gryrix disappear as he leaped off a rock and chased down one of his enemies. She saw no sign of Krel or Aryus but knew they had to be somewhere close, somewhere near the station. It was only when she caught sight of a dark shape between the fumes of field smoke that she had to pause and then stop.

Breathless, she stood there watching, uncertain if she had seen it right. And even if she thought she saw it right, her mind told her it was likely Krel or Aryus after all, stalking a hunter who was about to set his sights on a group of men hiding behind a fallen mech. Still, she couldn't bring herself to move, even as she heard Elise call to her. She waited, feeling like she was rooted to the ground and nothing in the world could move her. Watching the red smoke with acute focus, she saw a familiar silhouette; a massive black shape against a red screen.

With the fires and the setting sun, the sky lit up in a sea of orange and red that reminded Lana briefly of home. A wind blew the smoke into a thin twister and, in the red haze, Xerus stalked slowly out in the open. His eyes, a violent reflection of the blazing fires around him, focused in on the hunter, his face stuck in a twisted snarl. He bent his head and closed in on the hunter like a predator stalking its prey.

Something must have given him away because the hunter turned suddenly and drew up his weapon. In response, Xerus struck. Faster than Lana had ever witnessed, he took the hunter out, ripping into his throat, spraying blood. A memory came to her of seeing Xerus do the same to a soldier in a video before they were ever together. Seeing it now with her own eyes made her feel sick.

"Lana? Lana, we have to go," she heard Elise shout.

Lana didn't respond. She wasn't sure she even could. She

watched Xerus slaughter the hunter, pieces of armor and flesh spewing across the grass.

He's gone. He's gone, Lana, and you can't save him. You have to leave him and go.

She was shocked. Shocked and decidedly angered by this thought. This ugly, betraying, hopeless thought.

"No," she said aloud.

"What? What do you mean?" Elise said from beside her. "You can't stay, Lana. You're gonna get killed if you stay. Do you hear me?"

Xerus rose up and saw the men, his nostrils flaring, teeth bared. He started for them.

As soon as he took a step toward them, a shot went off, and the ground right at his feet sprayed dirt. As he looked around, so did Lana, and she saw some several dozen meters off, a sniper and his comrade up on a rocky hillside, his gun aimed in Xerus' direction. Xerus hissed, then turned back toward the men and took another step. This time, a bullet hit its mark across Xerus' back. He growled but didn't stop. The men huddled behind the mech, empty guns at their feet. With trembling hands, they drew knives.

"Dammit," Elise growled. "Nezka, pick her up, let's get out of here—"

"No," Lana said again, louder. She turned to Elise and fixed her with a piercing glare. "No. Go to the ship and keep any hunters back. I'm staying."

Elise looked at her, confused and concerned until she looked up and her eyes widened. "What is that vrisha doing?" She started forward and Lana stopped her. "Isn't that your guy?"

"I have to go."

"Lana!"

Lana squeezed her arm. She forced Elise to look at her. "I have to go to him. You'd do the same for Nezka." She glanced over at the ex-hunter, who watched her carefully. Elise looked at him, then turned back to Lana with a frown. "If you go out there..."

"I know." Lana smiled sadly. "Go."

Elise shook her head but stepped back. Nezka took Elise's arm and drew her close to him. He bowed his head to Lana as if he understood.

"Thank you. To you both." Lana bowed her head. Without looking back at them, she turned and stepped out into the open. She started at a walk that quickened into a jog and then into an outright run.

"Lana? Lana, can you hear me?" Xilya called from her techband, her voice a mere hiss. "Don't go to him, Lana, he will kill—"

Lana yanked her techband off and threw it. As she passed through a small layer of smoke, she covered her face and coughed but didn't stop or slow. She didn't look around her to see if any hunters were coming or if soldiers were going to fire on her. She looked only ahead to Xerus as she called out to him.

His eyes were still on the men as he had yet to see her. He bent his head low and exposed his fangs, ready to charge at them. Bullets hit his thigh and side but couldn't keep him back. Not from this prey. If a bullet hit the right place, however, Lana knew it could be fatal. And it was only a matter of time before the sniper made his mark.

Before Xerus could move on the men, Lana closed the distance. She got between him and the soldiers, putting out her arms to make him halt. With her now in his way, Xerus paused and stood very still.

"It's me, Xerus," Lana said softly. "It's Lana."

Xerus' pupils expanded and his nostrils flared.

"You know me." She stayed several feet away from him, refusing to move. Xerus didn't move either as he studied her. "Listen to me. You're sick, Xerus." She dropped her arms slowly. "And I should have done something sooner. I knew something was wrong, but I didn't think...didn't know." She shook her head and felt the sting of tears. She took deep breaths to keep her composure. She swallowed hard, took another deep breath, and stepped closer. Xerus let out a low growl, and she hesitated before taking another step. "I love you, Xerus. I know you don't understand that right now. But I do and will no matter what." She raised one hand toward him, and he hissed, but she didn't drop it. "You've gone through so much. But I didn't see it. Didn't understand. Even at Lazris. I just thought you were a tough warrior and nothing could harm you. I was an idiot, and I'm sorry."

Xerus bared his teeth at her and lowered his head. Lana knew he was ready to strike her. She lowered her hand slightly and forced herself to smile. "You've gone away from me now. Maybe I was too late...but I'm not leaving you still. I can't."

Tail weaving behind him, Xerus took a slow step toward her, his hand raised slightly, talons extended. Lana closed her eyes and tried not to flinch as she felt his sharp claws graze against her cheek. She opened her eyes slowly and saw him looking down at his hand, his head tilted. Her eyes fell to his fingers and there she saw blood. Her blood. As he stared down at his hand, Lana dared take another step toward him.

"Xerus...I—"

His hand shot out and encircled her throat. Unprepared, Lana got one decent inhale of breath before his hand tightened. Panicked, she gripped and clawed at his wrist as he drew her closer, his fangs sliding out from his upper lip, ready to bite down and tear her flesh from bone. Lana writhed in his grip as she felt herself lifted off the ground, struggling to stand on her toes. His face came closer, and she felt her vision slipping. Knowing she wouldn't be able to break his hold on her, she stopped herself from trying to fight. Instead, she slid her other hand up his arm, gripping his shoulder, then touched at his neck and his face, brushing her fingers over his fine scales.

"Xerus..." Her head lifted back as she opened her mouth to catch breath. "Come...back."

His pupils dilated and he blinked once. His hand loosened but didn't release her. Lana took a slow breath and slid her fingers down to his jaw, taking hold of his face, making sure he saw only her. Tears —or maybe it was blood—slipped down her face and along her chin, catching on Xerus' hand. Her body shook and a burning pain grew up her spine. Her head swam, but she pushed herself not to faint. If she did, she knew he would be lost to her for good.

She repeated her words, repeated his name over and over as if it were a single light out in a dark sea and it was his only way back. He didn't move. He didn't release her, but he didn't attack her either, nor did he look away.

"It's me. Come back, Xerus," she whispered.

He blinked again, and his face twisted in an expression that looked pained. His eyes focused on her, and he saw her. His mouth opened and shut, and his throat moved as if he were trying to speak.

"Lana," he said in a sharp exhale of breath. His eyes widened as if he were in disbelief.

Lana tried to nod her head. "That's right. I'm right here."

He released her immediately, making Lana fumble back. Her legs gave out, and she started to fall when Xerus caught her and steadied her. She took several deep breaths and gripped his arms. When she looked up, his expression was grim.

"What have I done?" he said softly.

Lana couldn't find the words. She shook her head and let out a whimper. He cupped her face in his hands, his eyes drifting to her throat, mortified.

"What have I done?" he hissed, more to himself than her. His gaze darkened with rage.

"No. No, Xerus, stay with me." She placed both hands on his face and forced him to look at her. The panic in her voice seemed to draw him back.

"Lana..." He closed his eyes and allowed her to trail her fingers along his face.

She let out a tiny sob and brought his head down to touch against her own. "Don't go, Xerus."

She didn't know if he had already slipped away again. He hardly moved, hardly made a sound. When she lifted her head from his, he tilted his up to look at her, and she sighed in relief, sure now he still saw her.

She smiled at him as he brushed away tears with his thumb. "My Lana," he said.

There came a dull popping noise from far off and the woosh of something flying fast. Lana saw the bullets hit Xerus first—one into his shoulder and another through the spikes along the back of his neck—before she felt a sharp, exploding pain against her head. Xerus disappeared and the world went dark. The only noise was the sound of a distant roar, a terrible scream like a raging storm. The only feeling was that of falling slowly into darkness, like falling through water. Then silence and nothing.

CHAPTER FOURTEEN

It was hard to gauge when she started to remember things. Or to decipher what was real or a dream. There was so much and, yet, so little that brought her in and out of consciousness. Sometimes the noise was hell. Voices all around her, doors slamming, feet running. She remembered the heat, a terrible fire that seemed to melt her. She remembered the cold that settled in her bones, a chill like death. She had no thoughts to wonder if she was dead. There was only the odd heightened sense of everything around her. The feel of metal on her back, the whispers she couldn't understand, the hands that lifted her and set her down several times. The whirring and clicking of some machine and the blinking of lights. She felt and sensed these things, but she couldn't respond to them. All she could do was feel.

She had no sense of time. It didn't seem to exist at all wherever she was. All there was of time was the moment that she was in. For all she could guess, it could have been seconds or years; it meant nothing. All she knew was that there were times of silence and peace and times of noise and chaos. If it was in her to observe such things, she would notice that one voice, in particular, drew her out of the dark more than others. A sometimes angry voice, or distraught; a voice in agony.

When she felt her body being touched by strange hands, she hardly noticed or cared. She felt like an empty shell, apart yet separate from herself. Only when she felt a rough, warm hand on her—a familiar hand—did she feel almost pieced together again. Almost but not quite.

She floated through that abyss for all of an eternity before she finally saw a light and came back to the surface.

* * *

Lana blinked and squeezed her lids shut, a dull pain settling between her eyes from the bright light above her. She moaned and turned her head away, unable to escape the light. There was a soft shifting noise followed by a heavy clinking sound to her left and, a few seconds later, a warm hand touched her arm. Lana slowly opened her eyes. Everything was fuzzy until she blinked a few times and could see the room she was in. A bare gray room with soft white lights above. She looked over to whoever touched her and felt her heart flutter, bringing her fully out of whatever sleep-induced state she had been in. She let out a small sob and took Xerus' hand in hers, squeezing it tight.

"Are we dead?" was the first thing out of her mouth. She looked around the room and thought it wasn't much for an afterlife, but if Xerus was here, then she had to be in some sort of paradise.

Xerus huffed. "I should hope not. This would be an awfully disappointing place to end up."

"Where are we?" Lana asked.

Xerus smiled. "Within the station. Safe." He brushed his thumb along her palm intimately, and his smile faded, a shadow passing over his eyes. "You're safe."

Lana looked down at his hand and saw on his wrist a thick metal cuff fixed with a heavy chain. She followed the chain and saw it linked to the large metal chair he sat in.

"What...?" Lana said.

Xerus' eyes flitted down to the chains. "Just a precaution."

Lana sat up, studying him closely. "What happened?"

Xerus closed his eyes, his lip twitching. "Where would you have me start?"

Lana thought for a moment. "When you woke up...were you...?"

Xerus opened his eyes and stared back at her. "I was myself. It wasn't a nice feeling to find myself locked up and not know where you were."

Lana swallowed hard, realizing her mouth was very dry. She coughed and looked down at her lap, her heart sinking with shame. "I'm so sorry. I didn't want to..."

"It was good that you did. I was more concerned about where you'd gone than I was about being locked up." He squeezed her hand. "When Xilya explained to me why I was where I was, it was hard to believe at first. Hard to come to terms with it, which brought me to be, ah...combative. I was determined to get out and get to you, thinking little of the fact that I was a threat. My only thought was to keep you safe. I grew terrified when I heard the hunters were coming and desperation led to a not so pleasant conversation with one of the crew who'd come to set out food."

"What did you say to them?" Lana asked.

Xerus tilted his head, looking a little guilty. "Something along the lines of stripping them of their status and their ability to work on a ship ever again if they refused my command to be set free. It was not a proud moment but I was—"

"Desperate," Lana finished with an exhale of breath.

Xerus bowed his head. "I exited the ship from there and set out toward this station. My mind was clear up until I saw the hunters and the men, then...I forgot myself. All I craved at that moment was to hunt and kill. I had lost all sense of anything else." He shut his eyes and flinched suddenly, as if in pain.

"Xerus?" Lana reached for him, concerned.

"It's all right." Xerus opened his eyes again. "When I saw you there before me, it was like...I didn't recognize you. I didn't see *you.* Couldn't comprehend who or what you were to me. And yet your voice, your touch, seemed so familiar. In a way, my desire to know it grew. And I couldn't turn away."

Lana felt her face wet again as a few tears slipped. She pursed her lips and nodded. "I wasn't sure it would even work. But I couldn't just leave you either. "

"A part of me is overjoyed you didn't while another wishes you had, if only for the fact that I might have killed you."

"I know." Lana closed her eyes and breathed deep. "I know."

His eyes turned pained as his hand lifted up to touch her throat gently. "You risked much, kissala. Too much."

"It was worth it to me to have you back," Lana said, taking his hand and resting it against her breast.

"And if I hadn't..."

"You did and the past is in the past."

Xerus sighed, pulling his hand back gently and placing it on her thigh.

"And after?" Lana asked.

Xerus closed his eyes, face twisted again with pain. "I saw you get hit. And watched you go down. I thought that would be the death of me. Instead of turning me toward my forgetfulness, it brought me back. I cared little of anything else then, though my rage was beyond anything I'd ever felt. It was the other warriors who came to my aid and who I ordered to take you. First, back to the ship to try and stop the blood loss. Then to the station per the other woman's suggestion."

"Other woman?"

Xerus' eyes half opened as if in a daze. "The human woman."

"Elise," Lana said.

Xerus bent his head. "She mentioned the technology they kept and the...gydas' medical skills. She believed they would give you a better chance."

Lana's brow knitted in confusion. "The station last I saw was being overrun...and the fires were consuming it." Her eyes widened. "The hunters. Did they...?"

"Gone," Xerus said. "The men took much of the heat but, with our team and theirs, many of the hunters perished or fled. Once they were gone, the people of the station took care of the fires. Still, a good portion of it was lost."

Lana looked down at her hands, her free hand slowly turning into a fist. Her memory began to clear as she recalled what happened before she'd fallen. The sniper and his bullets that had hit Xerus had also hit her. By the look of him, Lana could see he had been treated for his wounds. "And the soldiers who attacked us?"

"Dead. Aryus expelled those on the cliff while the men hiding in the field surrendered. Most didn't survive the attack."

"I tried to warn them." Lana squeezed her fist tighter, then relaxed. "I can't feel sorry."

"As you were recovering, the team destroyed the Xolis ships. Nothing can be salvaged from them now." Xerus flinched and hissed, shutting his eyes.

"What's wrong?" Lana said, reaching for him again.

"Just...a headache. Nothing you should worry about, I promise," he said, rubbing his knuckles between his eyes.

"You're still trying to fight it, aren't you? The Redsight," Lana said, growing more concerned.

Xerus dropped his hand and gazed back at her. "Yes. But not solely on my own."

"What do you mean?"

Xerus' hand grazed Lana's thigh once more, caressing, then squeezing gently as if to comfort. "The gyda helped in their way. I had been so terrified of losing myself again and, more so, of losing you, that as soon as our team came to my aid, I ordered Aryus to keep his weapon locked on me should I lapse at any time in the process of saving you. Once we came to the station, those who cared for you inquired as to why I had one of my own ready to take me out. I told them of my...sickness and asked that they lock me in a holding cell as long as I was near you and would be updated on your condition. While you recovered, I allowed them to scan and evaluate me. It was then they found the growth..." Xerus' face twisted in pain, and he looked back at her, ashamed. "They gave me medicine to help. It keeps me clear for the time being but with a cost."

"Could they not take it out?" Lana asked, hope stirring in her. "Maybe with their advanced equipment, they could operate and..."

"Not here," he replied. "They know little of our anatomy. It was one of our crew who had to aid them in spotting the abnormality in the first place. But perhaps back on Tryth...we will see."

Lana's heart sank. The thought that he would have to remain in pain so that he didn't lose himself was hard to bear. "We will find a way," she said. "I will do everything I can to keep you here."

Xerus took her hand and pressed it to his mouth, then held it against the side of his face. "I know."

Lana watched him for a long moment. She took in his pained expression and the chains on his wrists and, without real warning at all, let everything go. She burst into tears and covered her mouth to stifle the sobs.

"I thought...I'd lost you...Xerus...I'm sorry," she said through breaths. "I was...so scared."

Vrisha did not cry or have tears. But for all of their tough facade, they understood sorrow and felt it just the same. Perhaps it would have been considered a weakness to some vrisha to see one of their queens in such a state. But for a predomis and, specifically for Xerus, such an outburst of emotions from their mate affected them as well. Xerus reached for her and pulled her to him, burying his face in the curve of her neck, nuzzling hard against her. He let out several short, hissing breaths as his chest shook and his hold around her tightened.

"I'll never be far from you," he whispered in her ear. "I'll stay right here."

CHAPTER FIFTEEN

It took eight more days after she'd woken up for Lana to feel recovered enough to leave her room. Before that, she'd been on her feet a handful of times, all with assistance from medical staff and twice by Elise who came to visit her.

The first time, it was to help her into the shower. Just the short walk alone made her feel slightly dizzy and unbalanced. Even with her surgery and the medication they gave her, she still was healing from the initial concussion that brought on fatigue and a wave of nausea. Even with the lights dimmed to help her sleep, she experienced mild headaches. All was a small price to pay for the treatment they had given her for the severe head wound she'd sustained.

When she'd finally seen herself in the mirror after, she'd gotten a look at the damage for the first time. She had no thoughts about what to expect, but what she saw was of no surprise to her either. The braids she usually wore had been unraveled, leaving what hair she had to fall down one shoulder. At the back of her skull and around her left ear, they had cut and shaved away what hair had been in the way when they had brought her into surgery. A crooked Y-shaped scar curled around the back of her head, her left ear disfigured where they had tried to piece part of it back together. Sad as it was, the silver lining to it all was that many vrisha saw scars as a testament to their hard-earned battles. They would see such a mark as a symbol of her victory.

As relieved as she was that they had won over the hunters in the end, Lana knew much had been sacrificed. She learned most of Sythtec's soldiers had died, Jameson and his crew perishing on the wall while most of the others were killed in the field. Those who did survive were severely injured but were recovering slowly on their own. Mr. Tabara had disappeared some time after the wall was destroyed, when the hunters started making their way inside, his personal ship gone. It was assumed he had retreated back to Earth and wouldn't likely ever return.

The majority of the city had thankfully been spared, though several buildings had been severely damaged with one wall completely gone. Bo, along with the other officials of the city, were already working to repair what they could with what materials Sythtec had left behind. Those of the city had safely hidden in the various bunkers below ground, none found by any of the hunters who managed to get inside the city. Lana's team along with Nezka had done a full sweep to make sure none were hiding nearby, and Xilya had used the ship's drones to track several miles outside the station. When she found evidence of several hunters hiding out after they had fled, the team had gone out to take care of them.

Xerus, of course, had stayed behind. He had remained the majority of the time by Lana's side, even on those days when she did little but sleep. On one of her last days in bed, he'd asked to have the chains disconnected from his seat so that he could guide her to the shower himself. He'd sat by her and combed her hair out after, being careful to not graze the back of her skull too roughly with the sensitive skin.

On the days he wasn't beside her, it was so he could sleep, giving him some rest from the headaches which, some days, were so painful he could hardly focus. She worried the most for him on those days, reminding her how soon they needed to return home.

When the ninth day came, she had enough of lying around, and the nurses deemed it safe for her to be up once a few more tests showed her concussion healed and her symptoms fading. They allowed her to get up on her own and to dress back into her kelva pants and shirt. Abrohs and the other gyda doctors were confident Xerus no longer needed to wear the chains now that he'd been on the medicine long enough to quell any threats of a lapse in his control. Together, she and Xerus walked down the halls of the city medical facility and outside for the first time in many days.

The sun was bright and the air slightly cool. The sky was clear with not a cloud in sight. For a moment, Lana thought she was actually back on Earth. Only from the unique insects and birds of the planet, similar but still different to Earth's, did it remind her that she wasn't on her old home world, not even close. It took a moment for her eyes to adjust to the light. They led her over to the center of the city where they had attempted to make a small park. She sat down on a patch of grass underneath a low-hanging tree instead of choosing to sit at one of the bench seats, wanting to feel the grass under her hand. Xerus sat beside her, and they took to watching groups of people walk by, talking and laughing as if nothing had happened a week before. It was a pleasant scene, watching the gyda and her kind sharing moments together. She thought again about a time long ago when she imagined seeing such a sight. Of several different races mingling as one in some new governed territory. At the time, she had imagined such a place inside Earth's boundaries, perhaps on some civilian world where the aliens were melded into human society. But now, watching those around her, she saw a city untouched, with a society all their own. And it was much more refreshing.

"There was a time," she said, beside Xerus, who had his arm around her back, "when I wanted this more than anything."

He looked down at her curiously. "What's that?"

"To see you free among my kind and others, living life together."

She smiled up at him. "Back on Lazris before I knew about your mission, I wanted to bring you out of that cell and have you with me, living on some human world, maybe with a few other vrisha. It was a silly thought, the idea of you being around other humans, thinking they wouldn't be afraid or that things might change. For some, maybe, but most...not likely. I'd given up that dream long ago, happy to be part of the vrisha instead. Seeing this place though...it gives me hope. Maybe such things are possible here."

His hold on her tightened, bringing her closer. "Perhaps so."

"It would be hard. No one can get along forever. But it could be a start."

Xerus went quiet for a moment, his tail flicking gently beside her. "Do you wish to stay here?" he asked finally.

Lana shook her head. "No. Tryth is my home. With you and our haven." She shifted beside him, resting her hand on his leg. "But maybe...maybe for others, it could be."

Xerus tilted his head as he observed the people around them. "It would be rare for a vrisha to call another world their home. But it's not impossible."

Lana shrugged. "Things are changing. People can change."

"You have shown that to be true," Xerus said.

Lana looked up at him. "I was wrong to think I was the only one who could manage to do so. To set my fears aside and embrace what I'd come to love. It was naive and ignorant to think myself alone and above my own kind and to fear them because of it. I see that now." Lana thought of Elise and her hunter, of Aly far away with her child; and of Bo and the other humans of the station. "There are many who feel the same, who wish the same thing I did many years ago. Even if there are those who will still always look to fight and to conquer, there will still be us."

"There will always be us." Xerus nuzzled the side of her head, and Lana turned to kiss him. He grinned at her, pleased despite what pain he might be feeling. He took hold of her braid and rubbed it in his fingers as they continued to sit and watch and just be.

As the day went by, they took a small nap together, no one bothering to disturb them. Lana dreamed of sailing on a bright sea, with other boats around her, happy and carefree. When she and Xerus eventually woke, they went to take a walk toward the gates. Bo and Abrohs found them.

"I'm so glad to see you looking better, Dr. Hart." Bo smiled as she waved to them. "And Xerus."

"Thank you, again, for everything," Lana said.

"Happy we could help." She glanced at Xerus and nodded. "The both of you."

Xerus bowed his head to her and Abrohs. "I am grateful."

"We gave your x-rays and tests to your crew to take back home," Bo said.

"And my suggestion on the best way to combat the growth," Abrohs said quietly. "For your surgeons."

"Yes, I'm sorry we couldn't do more for you here, Xerus," Bo replied.

"What you have done is enough," he said. "I would rather have the pain to combat the illness than have nothing at all."

"I take it you plan to leave soon, back to Tryth?"

"As soon as we can, yes," Lana answered.

"You will be missed," Bo said sincerely. "I wish we could have met in better circumstances, but I'm so glad we could help after everything you did." She looked off in the distance as the sounds of drills and machines filled the air. "And now we can start over."

Lana looked around and saw men and women working to repair one side of a building destroyed by fire. She saw more people by the broken wall, taking pieces left on the ground to salvage. She noticed they didn't try to fix it up like they did the buildings. In fact, one group was breaking apart one side completely.

"You're tearing down the wall?" she said in surprise. "Why?"

Bo looked back at her and smiled. "We are done hiding. We will keep up a smaller barricade for the sake of wildlife until we grow, but if we are to expand into a true city, we can't keep up these walls. This world is too big and full of possibilities, and it's time we utilized it."

"You won't have much in the way of protection," Xerus observed.

"He's right," Lana said. "And with Sythtec gone, you'll have little aid..."

"We have all the resources we need here on XL-08, at least the bare essentials," Bo explained. "Gathering those resources and the energy needed to repair and create better equipment and materials will be harder, it's true, but it's not impossible. It will take more time, but we will manage." She glanced at Abrohs, then back at Lana. "As for protection...we have a few who were trained as soldiers before coming here. We could have them train others if need be. It's not much but...with the threat gone and the signal stopped, we'd like to believe we won't have to worry about another attack for a long time."

Lana locked eyes with Xerus, who remained quiet, likely thinking the same as her. They needed better than just a few retired soldiers. Even if the threat from Xolis was gone and Sythtec could no longer control them, there was still the government of Earth and its military that might come looking to colonize and overtake the planet, boundaries or no. And even if hunters never came looking again or if Xolis ceased to search, there was still the possibility of other threats. And with an expanding city looking to fill itself with various people, they needed someone to keep order.

A thought fluttered around in Lana's head as she considered their plans. She took Xerus' hand, turning back to Bo. "I think I'd like to talk to my people."

Bo nodded and, with a promise to talk again soon, left with Abrohs back to their research building while Lana and Xerus slowly made their way out of the city to their ship.

* * *

Lana gathered her team, including Elise and Nezka, to sit together, making a central fire on grounds just outside the city near to her ship and to Nezka's, who had resettled his own close by.

They ate a meal together first, from the extra provisions they'd saved, Lana happy to see everyone back together and thankfully in one piece. Some had acquired a few new scars and they showed them off. Krel boasted about his fights while Gyrix grumbled beside him about being rusty but grateful for his bombs which had helped to destroy the hunters' ships. Lana learned of Nezka's scars and how he healed quickly, and Elise explained how she had learned to fight so well. They filled Xerus in on the various elements of the battle he had missed and talked of what was to come. Mostly of home.

Lana noticed Xilya was quieter than usual as she stared at the fire. As the others talked quietly amongst themselves, Lana took the moment to sit by her. They didn't speak at first, just watched the flames flicker in the breeze, seeming to grow brighter as the sun began to sink below the trees.

"I am ready to face the council," Xilya said after a moment. She turned and gazed at Lana. "When we return home, I will accept whatever punishment you deem necessary for my crime."

"Your crime?"

Xilya turned back to the fire. "I betrayed your trust and command. I had promised to tell you of Xerus' condition, and I broke that. I had been afraid of him compromising the mission. Perhaps if I had told you right away, you wouldn't have gotten hurt."

Lana dipped her head as she too watched the flames. "You did what you thought you had to. I'm not happy about it, but I'm not going to punish you for it."

Xilya shifted beside her, tail flicking across the ground. "The crew knows what I did. And what I had planned to do. Even not understanding fully of Xerus' illness, they agreed I had overstepped myself in not telling you and trying to fix the situation without your decision. I will be shamed back home, but it is the price I will pay."

Lana looked around at Xerus, who was talking with Aryus, then around to the others. She looked over at her ship, then to the forest beyond. "Maybe there is something you can do for me instead."

"What's that?" Xilya asked.

Lana rose from where she sat and, in turn, the others grew silent as she caught their attention. Xerus stood and moved beside her as she reached for him, taking her hand in his.

"I know we are all ready to go home. Many of you are ready to move on to new missions and journeys. I command nothing more of you apart from this mission." She looked around at each of them. "So, I don't order this of you as your queen but merely ask you as a human seeking help. This world has a lot to offer, with good people looking for a better future. But despite our success, they are still vulnerable and need guidance. They need protection." She looked down at Xilya, who met her gaze. "I want those willing to stay to help keep them safe."

They each stared back at her, none saying a word. Xilya blinked once, then twice as she looked up at her, then steadily rose to her feet.

"I would be honored to help." She bowed.

Lana smiled. She looked back at the others and saw the sisters bow.

"We would help as well," Nix and Dyrsa said.

Aryus bowed. "As will I."

Gyrix scratched at his jaw, thinking. "We could stay until the people are on their feet and are able to obtain their own defense. But to stay permanently is asking too much. Once a vrisha's mission is successful, they do not tend to linger..."

"We could tell others to come," Krel said, standing. "From Tryth. They could have us spend a year or two, then rotate out. And, who knows, some vrisha might want to stay longer."

"No vrisha would call another world their home," Gyrix said.

"But some might."

He huffed. "Like who?"

"Me," Xilya said.

The others glanced at her curiously. Xilya turned to them and bent her head. "I would stay," she said. "I will learn all I must from the people and aid those who come. I could make a place in the city for those seeking myself and other vrisha for assistance."

"Like an embassy," Lana said, feeling her excitement growing.

"A what?" Krel asked.

"It's a place where those from another territory reside in a different territory outside their own home, " Elise chimed in. "To help those from their homeland—or world in this case—in the new territory."

"Still," Gyrix replied. "It will be difficult to convince others to come."

"Maybe at first," Lana said. "But I will talk to the council."

Gyrix tipped his head in a shrug, and Xilya turned back to Lana.

"This place could have more than just the vrisha," she said. "I've thought about it for some time now, since the fight ended. This world could also help my friends stuck hiding in Xolis."

Lana's eyes widened. "You mean have them come here?"

Xilya bowed. "I think it could be the right home they need. It is far enough from Xolis and is large enough to accommodate. Those of the city claim they wish to build a place with no more boundaries between races. If they are true in their word, I see no reason that they would object to my friends settling here."

"As long as no one followed them," Nezka said from across the fire. "You wouldn't want those in Xolis to catch their trail."

"They are well hidden," Xilya stated. "And those who join them can be thoroughly checked. I trust my friends are able to sneak those wanting to get out of the empire away safely. And besides, I have a feeling no one is going to be looking for them. As of yesterday, I received word from my friends that Nihl has fallen entirely. And many cities which the nillium ruled are revolting." She looked over to Nezka, her eyes reflecting the fire. "Including, I hear, the city your old master, Vesra, once dominated. With his and the nillium's hunters now defeated, I think it's safe to say no one is in a position to command or to track those fleeing Xolis."

Nezka's eyes narrowed as he considered her news. "He won't lose his city easily. He'd burn it to the ground before he'd allow someone to claim it."

"If that is true, then I will have to warn my friends," Xilya said. "Hopefully, some lives can be spared in the rebellion."

With that said, Lana looked over at Elise, who met her gaze. Elise placed a hand on Nezka's shoulder. "We would love to help, more than anything," Elise said. "But we have one mission we want to finish first. After that, we'd be glad to return."

"Where will you go?" Xerus asked.

"We look for my own kind," Nezka answered. "If there are any left."

"That sounds like a long mission," Lana said.

"Depends on how far and wide we look," Nezka said, taking hold of Elise's hand and knitting her fingers with his. "But yes, it may very well be."

"How long ago did you lose sight of your kind?" Gyrix inquired, studying the hunter.

"When I was very young," said Nezka. "I don't remember any of them. I was alone when I was found."

Gyrix seemed to think on that but said nothing more.

"I'm sorry to see you go but understand that you must," Lana said. "To the rest, I am grateful for your help. I think it's time for me and Xerus to return home. Come tomorrow, we will prepare the ship. Those who come with us should be ready. Those who stay should gather their things. We will talk to Bo tomorrow about having you remain here to guard them as well as speak with the council to bring aid."

"Just focus on getting home," Xilya said. "And fix your predomis. We don't want another incident like before."

Lana glanced at Xerus, giving him a sad smile. He was looking at Xilya with an expression of sly amusement mixed with annoyance. "It is good that you are staying here. My queen might be able to forgive your actions, but I won't forget your attempt to keep me detained while not informing her, despite the circumstances. I would challenge you if it were not below me to throttle one of low rank such as yourself."

"It is good that you go so that I won't experience such an embarrassment to my person," Xilya said honestly, though her eyes were also bright with amusement.

"We will do all that we can here, Risa," Aryus said. "While you're away."

"It's a pity it's such a small settlement," Krel mentioned as he observed the city from afar. Blue and yellow lights glowed out in the distance from the few buildings within. "Not even half the size of a small haven on Tryth. They'll have a lot of work ahead of them if they want to achieve a real city of impressive size, made to accommodate all."

Lana squeezed Xerus' hand as she gazed out toward the small city with its half-broken wall and few dozen buildings, several with burnt sides, to its simple lights and small park with a handful of trees.

She smiled. "It's a start."

CHAPTER SIXTEEN

They took off from XL-08 to travel back to Tryth two days later, this time with just her and Xerus and their crew.

Xilya, along with the sisters, Nix and Dyrsa, and Krel and Aryus, stayed behind on the planet to serve as the city's new guards. Before she and Xerus left, the team gathered what supplies could be of use in the new world, leaving enough resources for her, Xerus, and their crew on the return home. With careful precision, they took apart one of the call system communicators connected to the ship and rebuilt it to work along with the city's more advanced computers, allowing for contact to Tryth and beyond without the need of a ship. The council had been informed of the team's new mission and was willing to send out more ships when the time called for it. Until then, they were on their own.

Bo and the other city officials had accepted their stay with great excitement. Though some of the people looked on the vrisha with nervous glances and an air of deep caution, they remembered how they had fought for the city and so were quietly grateful. As much as they prided on their ideals of a society brought together by and tied together with different races and their cultures, even they knew the vrisha would be a challenge, and the fear of them would take time to settle completely.

As they had moved everything the team needed out of the ship and she and Xerus were preparing to leave, Lana said her goodbyes to Bo and the gyda and to her team but didn't think it would be the last time.

"You'll be back," Bo said as she hugged her. "I know it. Just to see how far we've come."

"You can count on it," Lana said as Bo released her. "Xilya says there are refugees from Xolis looking for a new home. I said I'd meet with them when they finally make it here."

"We will be waiting. And we will be ready," Bo said. "They won't be the only ones."

"I should think not, knowing how many might be living out there now." Lana glanced up at the sky and saw the dull light of a few close stars.

"We will remain wary of any unfamiliar ships as well as familiar ones that we aren't expecting," Bo assured her.

Lana knew she meant any military or government who might come looking as well as unplanned Xolis ships. "Are you planning to stay in contact with Earth, or will you cut ties for good?" Lana asked curiously.

"It's funny you should mention that." Bo wrung her hands nervously. "Though we weren't planning to, we decided to give one last company a chance. Well, they're more of an organization really, but their sponsorship and resources could double the city's expansion in several years."

Lana crossed her arms, trying not to look too critical. "Are you sure that's a good idea? After Sythtec?"

"We didn't think so either at first, but it was your friend, Elise, who recommended them."

Lana's brow rose. "That so?"

"Yes, Grayhart is the name. They are dedicated to sending out ships to explore advanced worlds. You might have heard of them. In return for the land to build a ship port, they are giving us a generous amount of aid and supplies."

Lana nodded. "Ah. Yes, I know of them. In that case...you should be all right."

"We will keep a close eye though, don't worry." Bo smiled her brilliant smile and offered her hand. Lana smiled and took it.

"It's been an honor, Dr. Hart. Safe travels." Bo shook her hand and started back toward the research lab. "Until next time!" She waved.

Back at the ships, before they were to take off, Lana found Elise there waiting along with Nezka, their ship ready to leave with Lana's own. Gyrix was with them, his things already transferred onto the hunter's ship. Instead of staying on the new world or returning to Tryth, he elected to go with the pair, to help in their search for more of Nezka's kind.

"It's been many years since I was a young warrior," Gyrix said to Lana the day they started to prepare to leave. "But on one of my first missions, I encountered a tribe that looked very much like this hunter. I think I could aid in their search if we return to the planetary system in which I found them last," he explained.

"It's good of you to help," Lana said. Gyrix bowed and said his goodbye before entering the ship. Lana turned to Elise, who waited by the ramp as Nezka started up the engines. She was dressed in a set of shiny black armor plates just like her hunter, with her gun clipped to her belt. Lana thought she looked every bit a warrior.

"Good luck to you both," Lana said. "Don't get into too much trouble."

Elise laughed. "With Nezka, I can't promise." She placed a hand on Lana's shoulder. "I'm glad you found us when you did. Sure, it wasn't the best circumstances, but I'm glad we could be here to help."

Lana nodded. She lifted her hand, grasping Elise's outstretched arm. "I am too."

Elise released Lana's shoulder and started up the ramp of the ship where Nezka was now waiting for her at the door.

"Will you really come back after?" Lana called over the hum of the ship.

Elise turned back. "You can count on it." She waved, then turned to her mate whose brilliant orange eyes gazed down on her with a look of adoration before he whispered something Lana couldn't hear. They embraced and kissed deeply before Elise entered the ship. Nezka noticed Lana and gave her a quick bow before he followed, and the door closed behind him.

When Lana returned to her own ship, she found Xerus waiting. He watched her as she walked toward him, and she fixed him with a smile. "Ready to go home?"

"I've never been more ready," Xerus said. He reached up to touch her, and Lana closed her eyes as his fingers grazed lightly over her face and around her ear as he brushed back a stray hair. She focused on the feel of his hand against her—a rough, warm touch she could never stop loving. She placed her hand on top of his, pressing her face to his palm, grazing her lips along his wrist.

She took his hand and led him into their ship. Once secured, they took off with ease and watched as the blue planet that resembled Earth grew smaller in size.

As the ship traveled in space, they remained together in their room for most of the trip, only leaving to check on the deck every so often. Xerus slept a lot, but Lana didn't mind as long as he was no longer in pain. She lay beside him and fed him when he woke, and when she did sleep, she dreamed of home. Not of her father's beach house, but of the garden on Tryth, and of their bedroom, and of the brilliant red and orange sky on the terrace.

* * *

It took a few days once back on Tryth to find the surgeons needed for Xerus' operation. The vrisha were not known for their medical skills like the gyda. They were such a versatile race that the need for a doctor was very uncommon and usually unnecessary. But a few of the dirra had talent in not just technology but in vrishan medicine. And the very best resided in a haven east of their own, ruled by Queen Mavika.

The surgeons looked over the tests and diagnosis the gyda had made as she and Xerus waited on what could be done. Xerus continued to take the medicine given to him, but it was running out quickly, and they needed to make a decision soon. On the fourth day of waiting, they took Xerus through their own set of examinations to determine what sort of procedure would work best.

The morning Xerus went through more testing, Lana sat in an open waiting room connected to a small balcony that looked out into a circular garden below. She stared down at the spiky plants and the druumils fluttering around them, trying to keep herself from pacing. It had been a couple of hours since he had gone into the secretive rooms of the vrisha hospital, or "the healing grounds" as they called them, and the longer he was inside the more she started to worry.

What if they can't help him after all? she thought. *What if he won't be able to be himself without the medicine?*

The thoughts were poison on her brain that she couldn't drown out. Her eyes turned for the door, and she rose, starting for them. She was determined to get answers without waiting a moment longer when the door to the other end of the room opened, and a small vrisha with pinkish-red skin walked out.

"Queen Lana." He bowed. From the slow sway of his tail and the bend of his head, she could see his expression was solemn.

Lana stopped before him. "Can you heal him?" she asked.

The vrisha surgeon looked up at her sharply. "It is possible." Lana had begun to relax when he continued, "However, there may be complications."

Lana frowned. "What kind of complications?"

"The growth creating his sickness is close to the nerves and vessels of his brain that are connected to memory, impulse and sight. There is also a chance of damage to the brain causing his body to fail."

"He could die?" Lana choked out.

The vrisha bowed his head. "It is a small chance. It is more likely he may have one of the other complications. He may lose some of his memory, be prone to more angry fits, or perhaps even lose some of his sight. It is uncertain which, or whether any might happen, but you should know it is possible."

Lana almost went to sit down, but she realized she was no longer near her seat by the balcony. "Oh," she said in a hiss of breath.

"He knows of these risks and is willing to still go through with the surgery, but he wants your decision first."

Lana looked beyond him to the door, imagining she saw Xerus standing there waiting. She thought it over once, twice, then glanced back at the surgeon.

"If he is willing...then I am with him," Lana said.

The vrisha bowed. "We can operate on him now. It may take some time but, if successful, shouldn't take more than a few hours."

Lana was hesitant. "Can I see him first?"

"If you wish."

Lana followed the vrisha surgeon back through the door and down a narrow hallway. They passed by several rooms until they came to one at the end. Inside, Xerus lay on his side atop a low table, surrounded by various vrisha-made tools and machines. Lana went over to him, crouching down to face him. She took his hand in hers.

"They said they can operate on you today but..." Lana could barely say the words.

"I know." He squeezed her hand. "I wish it could be easier." Slowly, he sat up to face her, and Lana buried herself against him. He stroked her hair gently. "But I will come out all the better in the end."

Lana nearly bit her tongue to keep herself from saying "what if." She released herself from him to fix her gaze with his. She took his face in her hands and kissed his brow.

"I will be right here. Just a room away. I'll be waiting," she said.

He took her hands and drew them to his mouth before placing them against his heart. "And I will come back to you. I swear it."

Lana smiled though she was afraid. She kissed him on the corner of his mouth, then looked to the surgeons who watched patiently close by. They bowed, and the small pinkish one led her back to the waiting room.

Lana remained there by the balcony, looking out over the garden as they went to work. The air smelled sweet from the blooming of the oorinda flowers down below. The day was hot, as were all on Tryth, but Lana hardly noticed. She let her mind wander as the hours ticked by. She thought of station eleven and those they left behind. Then she thought about her father and her time on Earth. She thought of Lazris, even, and everything she and Xerus had gone through and wondered if he would remember any of it after the surgery. And, as awful as it made her feel, she wondered if it would be a good thing for him to forget if it meant forgetting all the pain and terror, only to sacrifice everything they shared.

She knew no matter how much he might forget, he would always be hers. She laughed a little at the idea of him waking up to find her as his queen and the confusion it would bring, but she knew in her heart, even then he would stay.

Tears came with the laughter, and she let them fall. She didn't know how long she sat there staring off in the distance, crying or laughing all to herself, but she saw the light fading and the sun disappearing over the wall of the haven and knew the day was almost gone.

When the light was nothing more than an orange haze over the horizon, the door at the end opened, and the vrisha surgeon from before approached.

Lana didn't even rise from her seat as she followed him with her gaze and watched him stop before her. She looked up into his face and saw the glint in his eyes as he bowed his head.

"It is done."

* * *

They spent seven days at Mavika's haven so that Xerus could rest and so that they could monitor his condition. He was in too much of a daze in the beginning to say much, and he was asleep more than he was awake in those first few days. But after a time, his mind began to clear, and he became more coherent. They asked him questions to gauge how severely his mind might have been affected and were so far satisfied that he had suffered no major injuries in response to his treatment. When Lana had gone back to him after the surgery and had sat by him, he had stared at her for a long while, and she feared he didn't recognize her. It was only when he reached for her and took her hand that she realized he knew who she was.

She never left his side after that. She brought him food on the days he felt good enough to eat and washed his scales and horns until they shined. He complained little about being pampered by her and mentioned more than once how he wouldn't be so upset if she bathed him and fed him back home as well.

"Don't push your luck," Lana said one day as she filed his nails while they watched the sun pass by from the balcony of their guest room. Still, she couldn't help smiling. "But maybe on those days when I'm feeling generous."

"A queen's generosity makes her well-liked," Xerus said as he reclined in his seat, watching her carefully, his tail skimming across her back.

"Yes, but those who expect too much of her will take advantage," Lana said, fixing him with a critical gaze.

Xerus grunted, meeting her eyes with a sly, amused sort of expression. "I would never think to take advantage of your kindness, kissala."

"I should hope not."

"But it is well appreciated. I shall hunt down a *gris* and bring it back in your honor as a token of my gratitude."

"You will do no such thing!" Lana snapped, thinking of that awful poisonous, tentacled beast and the many vrisha who'd died trying to hunt it. "If you wish to honor me, you will not put your life in danger ever again."

"Ah, that, I can't guarantee."

"Xerus."

Xerus smiled down at her with a sorry sort of expression. "Only for you would I ever. Though it will be difficult on our future missions to keep from such a risk."

Lana went quiet, her gaze falling. She didn't respond at first as she focused on the sharp nail of his thumb. After a moment, she said, "I was thinking that maybe...maybe we could stop now."

"Stop what?" Xerus asked.

"Missions." She glanced up at him, then quickly looked away. "At least take a very, very long break."

"You wish to retire?"

"No....and yes," she said. She paused in her filing and looked back at him. "I'm not saying we have to quit entirely but...honestly, I'm tired, Xerus. And I want to focus on home now. Just home."

Xerus studied her, and Lana could see he was thinking it over.

"I know we can't stop entirely as it's a vrisha's duty, but I want to remain here for a while. And focus on our haven and our family." Lana went still as the words spilled out. "I mean...in our own way," she said nervously. "If I could have forever, I would, but if we must take more missions, I don't want them to involve risking any more than we already have. You've done so much, Xerus, for this world. And you've had to deal with the aftereffects. I don't want you to have to deal with more. Do you understand?"

Xerus stared at her for a long moment, then gestured for her to stand beside him. Lana rose from her seat and allowed Xerus to take hold of her arms.

"I understand," he said and smiled. "If it is what you desire...then it shall be so."

"You really mean that?"

"I do," he said. "And perhaps it's time we worked solely on what we have here."

"I'd really like that," Lana breathed. She lifted a hand and brushed her fingers along his jaw. "Just you and me."

Xerus smiled, showing off his fangs. "I remember when you were just a frightened but ambitious woman, determined to get through to me, an unmoving warrior. You are truly beyond anything I could have imagined, my Lana."

Lana grinned, then brought her face down to brush her mouth against his. "I am full of surprises." She straightened. "Just to keep you guessing."

"Another thing I am deeply grateful for." He took hold of her waist and brought her down to sit on his lap. Lana curled into him, placing a hand behind his neck to grasp at his spikes.

"And for that, you need no other surprises," she said. "I think we've had enough for the both of us these last few weeks."

"To that, I can agree." Xerus nuzzled her neck. "I am ready to return to our haven."

Lana took a deep breath, filling her nose with his coffee-like scent, then exhaled slowly. "And to stay."

EPILOGUE

Xerus

The world was a brilliant blue sphere. It glowed like the gems found in the tikari caves. So different from his home yet still a treasure to see. From the window, he watched as the world grew closer. Their ship slowed as it readied its descent into the planet's atmosphere.

His mate had said it looked near to her old home world—Earth. He hadn't had the chance a year and a half ago to truly appreciate it when they'd left to return back to Tryth, but he took that chance now to study every landmass and cloud along its shape. It could never compare to his home—nothing ever could—but he felt a sort of fondness for this place, even if the memories of it were not so happy.

A hand rested on his arm, and he didn't need to look around to know whose it was.

"It gives me chills," Lana said beside him. "It will be a real sight to see the glow of a huge city down there someday. Or maybe even several. And we know how it all got started."

"Will it be like Earth?" Xerus asked.

"By its structures, maybe." Lana squeezed his arm. "But the people? Not a chance."

"It will be better."

"Let's hope so," she said.

Xerus turned to his mate, who looked back at him, her mouth curling upward. He could see the excitement in her eyes. He felt it too in a way.

"We are prepared to land," said a crewman at the terminal.

As the ship made its descent, they watched as a pattern of white and silver buildings appeared past a set of clouds.

"It looks like they've done a lot in just a year," Lana said. The walls were gone and what had once been a caged-in community was now spreading across the forest-side and down near into the valley below. As the city grew closer, they could see the people looking up toward them. When the ship settled onto an open space where a shipbed had been erected, he and Lana started toward the door. The light spilled out from the exit, making him blink several times as he adjusted to the brightness outside. They stepped off the ship and were quickly greeted by familiar faces. Among the human researchers and the gyda, he saw Xilya and their old team. The human official, Bo, ran to Lana first and hugged her before giving him a short bow.

"I'm so glad you could be here," she said with a wide smile.

Xilya approached behind her, along with the young warrior Krel, then the sisters and Aryus. They each bowed and welcomed their return.

"You look well," Xilya said to both of them. She glanced toward Xerus. "You were able to recover, I take it?"

"Yes. Some of my memories, I found, had been scattered, but it was a small price."

"A small price indeed. I'm glad you are better," she said. "We've greatly anticipated your arrival."

"And you're just in time. The ships are on their way now," Bo mentioned from beside them. "Those from Xolis are nearly here."

The team led them across the shipbed toward the city, and Xerus paused as he saw a familiar ship parked close by.

"What is it, Xerus?" Lana asked, stopping.

He gestured to the ship, and Lana followed his hand. Her eyes widened.

"When did they get here?" Lana asked Bo.

"Only a few weeks ago. Come see!"

They followed her and the others into the city, to its core, where the park he and Lana had once laid in had grown and was larger and more open than before, with a new set of trees surrounding its edge.

Under the shade of one tree, Xerus could see a small group talking quietly. They were nothing more than shadows until a few turned in their direction, and glowing, orange eyes stared back at them. As he and Lana approached, Gyrix appeared from another set of trees and greeted them.

"Predomis, Risa." He bowed. Xerus noticed he had a few new scars across one arm and along his chest.

"It seems your mission was a success and not without its rewards," Xerus commented.

"It was, and yes, one of my most...interesting missions ever. I think the vrisha might have found a match in these fyriens."

Lana made a noise beside him and grabbed his arm as another woman, dressed in black armor, came out from the shadow of the tree and ran toward them. Lana met her halfway and they embraced.

"Elise, I didn't think I would see you!" Lana said as she released her.

"I didn't think I would be back in time either," Elise said. She smiled as the hunter Nezka broke from the shadowed group to join them. His eyes narrowed on Xerus as he grinned, and Xerus returned the expression with his own challenging smile.

"So, you found your people after all," Xerus said. "Despite the odds."

"It wasn't as easy as it might seem," Nezka replied. "If it weren't for Gyrix, it would have been a bigger challenge. I have his guidance to thank. Without his memory, tracking them would have likely been impossible." He twisted back toward the tree and tapped at his ear.

Out from the shade of the tree, the group of what Gyrix called fyriens stepped out into the light. There were eight in total including what Xerus assumed were three females along with two fledglings—one male, one female.

"So few," Lana said. "Was this all?"

"No." Elise shook her head. "There were more, but these were the only ones willing to come back with us. The fyriens are...a very cautious race."

The fledglings looked around them nervously. The female tugged the male child's ear, and he snapped at her with sharp teeth. They ran out and started to fight, a dagger flashing in each hand, but no one stepped in to stop them.

"Guess fighting is in their blood too," Lana commented.

Elise laughed. "Oh, no it's in their soul. If I didn't have on all this gear, I could show you the scars. They felt bad when they realized I couldn't regenerate skin or heal as quickly, so they left me alone after that."

"What kept them from outright killing you?" Xerus asked curiously.

"I was persuasive," Nezka replied.

"With his fists, more or less." Elise shrugged. "And, to be fair, Gyrix intimidated them. Which granted us more respect. "

Xerus couldn't help grinning with pride. "It takes seeing a predator above them to become more humbled."

Nezka snorted. "It only takes one fight to see who is better matched."

Xerus tilted his head. "Do they need a demonstration?"

"Oh, enough, honestly!" Elise said. "For once, I am truly sick of fighting."

"Me as well," Lana agreed, giving him a stern look.

"Another time." Nezka smiled.

"We've talked of building a proper sparring pit," Xilya said. "I have promised my nillium friend a fight when he arrives. I think we could add the fyriens into the mix."

The fyriens and the vrisha team glared at one another in silent agreement.

"That will have to wait," Bo said from nearby. "Once we have the Xolians settled in. Speaking of which..." She brought up a small pad displaying a map. "They are in the solar system now. We are having them land in the valley as their ships are too big. Come with us."

They made their way to the edge of the city. Many of the trees that once made up the forest between the city and the valley were gone, leaving only a few scattered between buildings and paths. They stopped on the steps that led down into the open field, and Xerus could see the whole valley beyond.

The memory of running through the forests and cutting through hunters as he made his way toward the station, toward Lana, struck him. He closed his eyes and recalled with great detail his blind "hunt" and was eternally grateful that he had been brought back from those dark, savage depths. He silently thanked Rikasha and Veradis that he had his mate still by his side. His beautiful queen. He opened his eyes and turned his head to look at her, only her. Even as he heard the ships coming down and saw her face light up as they descended, he looked only to her. And he felt bliss.

* * *

The Xolians had finally come. The one they called the night prince—Ryziel—led his refugees into the city alongside his mate, Aly, and their child. The other human woman—Sarah, Xerus was told—had wept as she set foot on the place they now called Terra Centra. A better, more suitable name than XL-o8. The city kept its name of New Haven. And to those who came seeking a home, it truly was the safest place they felt they could be. Xerus saw the many races that had joined Ryziel in his exodus. Species of all shapes and sizes and—to a few who were surprised—some of the nillium themselves who had denounced the ways of Nihl and Xolis and were also looking for a new beginning.

"We are deeply happy and grateful to call this world home," Ryziel said. "And we will do all that we can to make it a place of unity."

A small creature they called Nar grumbled something from behind him as he fixed the goggles over his eyes. A few others looked cautious themselves, and Xerus knew with so many different people, unity wasn't going to come easily or quickly. But in the others, there was hope and, in that, there was the possibility of working things out together. Xerus had seen his share of conflict and war, but he also knew the universe was full of endless possibilities. And of impossibilities that turned into realities. He'd seen that truth come to light in his bonding with Lana, and he saw it in the other women who had dared to call these dark, inhuman men their mates. Anything was possible.

The universe really was an odd and terrifyingly beautiful place.

Don't miss Vrisha Warriors. A new series in the Dark World Mates Universe!

Xora (Vrisha Warriors)

OTHER BOOKS BY OLIVIA

Dark World Mates

Heart's Prisoner
Dark's Savior
Shadow's Chosen
Heart's Keeper

Vrisha Warriors

Xora
Axrel
Vrexus
Xeda

Sidonions

Shade's Embrace
Draka's Heat

**Sign up for Olivia Riley's Newsletter for updates on
new releases, and promotions.**

Olivia's Newsletter
https://oliviarileyauthor.com

ABOUT THE AUTHOR

Olivia Riley loves the frightening possibilities of deep space, where dark heroes and brave heroines reside. She also loves chocolate and gaming.

Instagram: oliviarileyauthor

Facebook: OlivaRileySFR